THE FORTUNES OF TEXAS

*Follow the lives and loves of a complex family
with a rich history and deep ties
in the Lone Star State.*

THE WEDDING GIFT

The town of Rambling Rose, Texas,
is brimming with excitement over the
upcoming wedding of five Fortune couples!
They're scheduled to tie the knot on
New Year's Eve, but one wedding gift
arrives early, setting off a mystery
that could send shock waves through the
entire Fortune family...

Brian Fortune has no interest in catching the
wedding fever that has overtaken the rest
of his siblings. Emmaline Lewis is six months
pregnant and isn't ready to trust another man,
much less a playboy Fortune with commitment
issues. But after an unexpected New Year's
Eve kiss, their friendship quickly escalates into
something neither of them had planned on...

Dear Reader,

I love New Year because it's such a time of fresh starts. So kicking off the 2022 Fortunes of Texas is a huge honor. Especially when the story involved two characters who needed a fresh start in life more than they even realize.

Emmaline Lewis has big plans for the coming year with a baby on the way, although she never expected to be a single mom. Already she loves her child and the life she's building in Rambling Rose after taking over her grandfather's antique shop. Her focus is on the future, but one midnight kiss from a stranger sets her off on an entirely unexpected journey toward love.

The kiss is just as monumental for Brian Fortune, who is just visiting Rambling Rose for a big family wedding. He's a confirmed bachelor and has no plans to settle down in the small town that his twin brother now calls home. When he and Emmaline begin working together to untangle the mystery of a cryptic message hidden inside one of the wedding gifts, he can't deny the connection he feels to the beautiful mom-to-be. Brian and Emmaline both have past hurts to overcome, and they'll have to decide how much of their hearts they want to risk for each other.

I found so much hope and joy in their story, two things I think we can always use more of in the world. I'd love to hear from you, as well. Find me at michellemajor.com.

Happy reading!

Michelle

Their New Year's Beginning

MICHELLE MAJOR

HARLEQUIN

SPECIAL
EDITION

Special thanks and acknowledgment are given to Michelle Major for her contribution to The Fortunes of Texas: The Wedding Gift miniseries.

Recycling programs for this product may not exist in your area.

ISBN-13: 978-1-335-40827-3

Their New Year's Beginning

Copyright © 2021 by Harlequin Books S.A.

This edition published by arrangement with Harlequin Books S.A.

For questions and comments about the quality of this book, please contact us at CustomerService@Harlequin.com.

Harlequin Enterprises ULC
22 Adelaide St. West, 41st Floor
Toronto, Ontario M5H 4E3, Canada
www.Harlequin.com

Printed in U.S.A.

Michelle Major grew up in Ohio but dreamed of living in the mountains. Soon after graduating with a degree in journalism, she pointed her car west and settled in Colorado. Her life and house are filled with one great husband, two beautiful kids, a few furry pets and several well-behaved reptiles. She's grateful to have found her passion writing stories with happy endings. Michelle loves to hear from her readers at michellemajor.com.

Books by Michelle Major

Harlequin Special Edition

Welcome to Starlight

The Best Intentions
The Last Man She Expected

Crimson, Colorado

Anything for His Baby
A Baby and a Betrothal
Always the Best Man
Christmas on Crimson Mountain

The Fortunes of Texas: The Wedding Gift

Their New Year's Beginning

The Fortunes of Texas: The Hotel Fortune

Her Texas New Year's Wish

The Fortunes of Texas: Rambling Rose

Fortune's Fresh Start

Visit the Author Profile page
at Harlequin.com for more titles.

To all the readers who believe in fresh starts
and second chances. Keep believing!

Prologue

Christmas Eve

"Again, Uncle Brian, again!"

Brian Fortune grinned as he lifted first his nephew Toby and then the shyer twin, Tyler, up over his head so that the boys could pretend to be Santa's reindeer taking off for their long Christmas Eve journey.

"You're going to regret that when the extra cupcake each of them snuck after dinner makes a second appearance." Brady, Brian's twin and the boys' adoptive father, placed a gentle arm around the shoulders of his fiancée and the boys' adoptive mother, Harper Radcliffe, as she giggled.

"Nobody saw us take those cupcakes," Toby said, his eyes wide.

Brian placed Tyler onto the thick carpet of the meeting room in the Hotel Fortune where their extended family had gathered for a lively white-elephant gift exchange among the adults. Each child had also received one special pre–Christmas morning gift, although Brady's five-year-old twins were clamoring for more.

Tyler sidled closer to his brother, the same way Brian always had with Brady when they'd been that age. "We ate 'em under the table, so nobody saw."

"I saw," Brady said with a knowing nod. "You know who else saw? Santa Claus. Did you two forget the jolly old guy sees everything this time of year?"

Brian bit back a smirk as Tyler's expression turned stricken. "Is he going to put us on the naughty list?" Tyler's chin trembled ever so slightly, while Toby straightened his shoulders like he was ready to go to battle with an army of elves to prove that he and his brother deserved to remain on Santa's nice list.

"Of course not," Harper answered immediately, crouching down and opening her arms. Brian couldn't imagine bending that way could be comfortable with her pregnant belly. Harper was due to give birth in a little over a month, but that didn't stop the twins from rushing forward for comforting hugs. "You're the best boys ever, and Santa knows that."

"Harper is right," Brady said, ruffling Tyler's brown hair. "But just to be on the safe side, why don't the two of you help with cleaning up the wrapping paper and bows? That will get you some extra last-minute nice points for sure."

"Okay," Toby said and led his brother toward the towering spruce tree that dominated the corner of the room.

With a gaggle of Fortunes and their respective partners and families in attendance tonight, the room buzzed with energy and cheer. In addition to Brady and Harper, there were several other happy couples in the room. Their older brother, Kane, and younger sister, Arabella, had also found love in Rambling Rose. They'd be joining Brady and their cousin, Megan Fortune, as well as Wiley Fortune, in a massive wedding on New Year's Eve, so tonight seemed particularly festive with everyone in high spirits.

They'd had a casual meal catered by the hotel's flagship restaurant, Roja, which had been started by Megan's sister Nicole. The gift exchange followed. There were still discarded bows and strips of cheery paper strewn around the room. Tyler and Toby dutifully began collecting scraps and dropping them in the large trash can pushed against one wall.

"I was joking about the naughty list." Brady lifted his hands in supplication as Harper turned to him, her delicate brows raised. "I definitely didn't mean to freak them out."

"Our boys need to get home and to bed," Harper said gently and then placed a hand on her stomach. "This little one and this mama, too."

Brian nodded when her gaze tracked to him. "Brewing up a baby is hard work, huh?"

Brady sputtered as Harper gave Brian a wide smile.

"A baby isn't like a cup of coffee or a pint of Guinness," his twin said with an eye roll.

"It's kind of like that," Harper said, rising onto her toes to give her soon-to-be husband a quick kiss on the cheek. "I know what Brian meant."

Brady relaxed and pulled Harper closer to his side. Brian had noticed since arriving in the small town of Rambling Rose, Texas, some definite changes in his brother. There was a sweetness and softening he hadn't expected in charismatic Brady. Particularly apparent was the fact that he couldn't seem to keep his hands off Harper.

Their affection was natural and unforced, but Brady seemed to unconsciously find reasons to touch her. A hand on the small of her back or pushing an errant strand of hair away from her face. They had an obvious connection, and Brian was still getting used to his twin brother being so smitten.

A sudden pinch in the vicinity of his heart had Brian rubbing two fingers against his wool sweater. It was great to see his brother so happy, although the changes in Brady's life also had resulted in changes that Brian hadn't anticipated.

He would have never expected his twin to take to the role of father so naturally. The whole family had been shocked when Brady had been named guardian of his best friend's twin boys after the tragic accident that killed Toby and Tyler's parents.

Then Brady's move to Texas from New York, along with the boys, had left Brian on his own. He was an adult living his own very successful life as a brand-and-marketing manager for a respected ad agency, but his twin had always been nearby, and he felt the physical distance more than he cared to admit.

"Harper's right, as usual," Brady said, giving her shoulder another squeeze. "The boys are going to be up at too-damn-early o'clock tomorrow morning, so they need to get to bed now." He pointed a finger at Brian. "You've got the supplies for tonight?"

"The biggest bags of glitter and Milk Duds

you've ever seen," he answered. "And crescent cutouts to leave reindeer footprints all around the house."

"It's such a cute idea, Brian," Harper told him. "The boys are going to get such a kick out of seeing reindeer droppings in the yard. You're a good uncle."

"No biggie." Brian shrugged, embarrassed to feel his cheeks heating under her praise. It was silly, but he didn't like being the center of attention. Still, the boys were way more fun than he'd expected, and he was having a great time spoiling them during his extended stay in Rambling Rose. He'd seen a clip online about how to make it look like Santa and his reindeer had really stopped by the house, and offered to get creative for Tyler and Toby.

"You'll be a good godfather, too," Brady added.

"Right," Brian said, shifting to look out at the crowd of Fortunes around the room. He'd agreed to stay in Texas until the new baby came and to act as his niece or nephew's godparent. He still wasn't sure he was the best choice of Brady's five siblings. Five-year-old twin boys could be entertained with candy and underarm farting noises, but a newborn would be uncharted territory for Brian.

Territory he didn't exactly relish moving into.

"Daddy, there's another present," Toby shouted

as he and Tyler returned, each of them holding one end of a large box. Brady smiled at the boys, and Brian knew how much it meant that they'd started calling him "Daddy" and Harper "Mommy". He never would have pushed them because he always kept their late parents in mind, but Brady and Harper truly loved the boys as their own. They were a family. "Uncle Kane found it under the tree."

Brian watched as his twin took the box with a frown. Harper glanced at Brady, who darted a questioning gaze toward Kane, their eldest brother. Kane lifted his hands as if he had no idea where the wrapped gift came from.

"The paper isn't very holiday-ish, and it's addressed to Brady and me," Harper said as she touched a finger to the large cream-colored ribbon that encircled the box.

"It has wedding cakes and champagne flutes printed on it," Brian observed. "Looks like someone sent an early wedding present."

Brady placed the box on a nearby table. "Why would we get a gift at the hotel?"

"Well, the big occasion's going to take place here," Brian pointed out.

"In a week," Brady answered.

Brian glanced around the room, for a moment finding it difficult to believe that soon there would be even more Fortunes gathered for the black-tie event, which promised to be elegant, romantic and lively.

"Can we open it?" Toby asked. "It's so heavy. Maybe there's treasure in it."

"Or a toaster," Brian suggested.

"We got a toaster," Tyler told him, tugging on the hem of his sweater. "'Member? You burned the frozen waffles yesterday."

"Good point, Ty." Brian placed a hand on the boy's thin shoulder. The kid reminded him so much of himself as a young child.

"We can open it," Harper said as she lowered herself to one of the chairs at the table. She held up a hand as the twins surged forward. "If you promise to go home right after with no fuss. We need to put out the milk and cookies and get to bed before Santa comes."

"Okay," the boys said in unison.

It was sweet how excited the two kids got at unwrapping gifts. They'd clapped for every person who'd received a present tonight, their excitement not dimmed in the least by whether the recipient opened a pair of socks or a bottle of wine.

After a nod of agreement from Brady, Harper made a show of tugging at the ribbon. "Oh, this is a tough one to open. Maybe the two of you could help me?"

Toby and Tyler didn't need to be asked twice. They attacked the box like they were indeed unearthing valuable treasure.

Harper laughed, but her smile dimmed as they pushed aside the tissue paper inside the box to reveal…a horse.

The bust of a horse's head, to be exact.

"Maybe whoever sent it should have stuck with a toaster," Brady muttered.

Harper pulled the sculpture out of the box and held it up so they could all get a better look, then handed the bust of the horse to Brady. She leafed through the tissue paper and peered more closely into the box. "There's no card," she said. "Is there anything stuck to the sculpture that would give a hint as to who sent it?"

"No." Brady shook his head. "There's a plaque at the base, but all it says is 'True beauty lies within.'"

"Definitely in this case," Brian said with a chuckle, "because this horse is ugly."

Harper made a face. "I hate to be an ungrateful bride-to-be, but Brian is right."

"Um, maybe it's a blessing we don't know who sent it," Brady said as he turned the sculpture to stare into the empty slits where the horse's eyes should be. "It's creepy." The sculpture was made of copper, dyed to look like it had a vintage patina. Or maybe it was an antique. It certainly looked old to Brian. The horse's carved mane gave the impression of being windblown, and its harsh features appeared almost bewitched.

"Maybe it's possessed," he said under his breath.

"Or cursed," Brady added with an exaggerated eyebrow wiggle. "I'm getting a Temple of Doom vibe from this thing."

"Or maybe someone is making you an offer you can't refuse," Brian suggested with a grimace.

"If you're going to make a *Godfather* reference, then I'm glad we opened the thing here and didn't have to open it in our bedroom."

"Is it haunted?" Toby asked, sounding intrigued.

Tyler moved back several paces until he bumped into Brian's legs. "I don't like it," he said, his voice shaky. "Put it back. Please, Daddy. Put it in the box. I don't want that in our house."

The boy's voice was growing louder and more panicked with every word.

"It's okay, sweetheart," Harper said soothingly.

Tyler shook his head, then reached behind himself and placed a death grip on Brian's leg.

"Let the real, soon-to-be godfather get rid of that thing." He held out his hands as Brady quickly stuffed it back into the box.

"You can't get rid of it," Harper told him. "Not until we find out who sent it."

"Someone with terrible taste," Brady told her.

"But we need to send a thank-you note," she insisted as she hoisted herself to her feet.

"I hate it," Tyler whispered.

Brian didn't know why the kid was so affected by the sculpture, although the weird vibes from that kind of gift couldn't be denied.

"It's okay, Ty," Toby said, patting his brother's arm. "Let's go get one last cookie while Uncle Brian takes care of the horse."

"One cookie between the two of you," Harper said.

It was a testament to how in need of soothing Tyler was that Brady and Harper weren't arguing about the boys topping off the night with yet another dessert.

Brady and Brian shared a look, and Brian didn't need his twin to speak in order to understand the message he was trying to convey. "I'll take care of it," he told his brother and Harper.

Brady nodded. "Thanks, Bri."

"Please don't throw it away," Harper added. "We need to find out who sent it."

"Harper's right," Brady agreed, scrubbing a hand over his jaw. Brian could read the tension in his brother's face. He didn't like to see the twins upset. "Although it's clear that thing will never have pride of place in our home."

"It might keep the boys from sneaking out when they get older," Brian suggested with a wink. "Set up the horse to guard the front door. They wouldn't dare cross that threshold."

"Good point," Brady answered. "We might have to keep it hidden away in the basement until then. Right now, I'm putting you in charge of figuring out where and who it came from. Think of it as best-man duty."

"I thought I was in charge of the strippers." Brian chuckled when Harper reached out and lightly smacked his arm. "Just kidding, Harper. We all know my twin is already an old married man in his heart."

"Proudly," Brady agreed, dropping another kiss on Harper's head. They shared a look of mutual adoration that sent another wave of unwelcome aching through Brian's chest.

He took the box to his car before the twins returned, inhaling deep pulls of the clean Texas air. Lifting his gaze to the sky, he marveled at the cascade of stars twinkling above him. Sure, he'd seen stars in Buffalo, the city where he'd been born and raised and still lived, but maybe there was truth to the notion that everything was bigger in Texas. The expansive sky had him catching his breath.

And when one bright light darted down toward the earth, Brian had the fleeting idea to make a wish for his own future happiness. Something about seeing several of his siblings settled and in love made him wonder if his solitary life was all it was cracked up to be.

Then he glanced at the corner of the horse's ear poking up from the tissue paper. Fanciful notions weren't for men like Brian. He slammed shut the trunk on his sleek BMW and turned back toward the hotel. He'd be in Rambling Rose for a few weeks before returning to his normal life and back to gaining control of his emotions.

Chapter One

The new year was only twenty minutes away, but Brian felt like the countdown was ticking by in slow motion. He rubbed a hand along the back of his neck and tried to ignore the fact that his cheeks hurt from smiling so much as he made his way to the bar situated along the far wall of the large room in the Hotel Fortune. Couples danced in the center of the room, led by their sister, Arabella, and her new husband, Jay Cross. People who weren't cutting a rug met and mingled along the perimeter. Wiley Fortune, the cousin who'd led much of the more recent construction in Rambling Rose, bent close to his bride, Grace, whispering something in her ear that made her giggle. A sense of happiness and celebration infused the entire scene.

The wedding had gone off without a hitch, and Brian had taken great pleasure in teasing Brady about his obvious nerves as they'd waited for the ceremony to begin along with the four other grooms. Brian still had trouble wrapping his mind around the fact that both Brady and their brother Kane were now married men. But Kane seemed just as happy with his new bride, Layla, as Brady did with Harper, so Brian could only wish them all the best.

"You've got twin boys and a baby on the way," Brian had reminded his twin. "Most guys think that's the hard part. Making it official is just the icing on the cake."

Brady hadn't argued. There was no doubt of his love and commitment to Harper and the family they'd already created.

But then he'd surprised Brian by talking about how he sometimes worried whether he deserved a woman as amazing as Harper to call his own. It was a definite role reversal for Brian, the younger twin by two minutes, to be giving relationship advice to his confident brother.

In doing so—reminding Brady about the bond he and Harper shared along with the two boys who'd brought them together—Brian had felt the now-familiar ache in his chest grow stronger. Brady had met Harper when he'd hired her as the twins' nanny, so it was unlikely Brian was going to have the same romantic luck as his brother.

His twin's life had taken a remarkably different path from Brian's, and he would swear up and down that he didn't actually want what Brady had.

But it was getting harder to ignore the emptiness inside him at being left behind—even figuratively.

He dug in his pocket for the roll of antacids he'd started carrying, muttering a curse when his fingers brushed the remnants of an empty wrapper. He wasn't sure the tablets helped, but how else could he explain the way his chest burned?

At the bar, he took a seat next to his only remaining single sibling, Joshua, who was talking to Stefan Mendoza. Stefan's brother Mark had been another of the grooms at the big event, marrying Brian's cousin Megan. There were two etched glasses of whiskey in front of Josh, and without missing a beat, he slid one toward Brian.

Brian immediately threw it back, blowing out a breath as a trail of fire seared his throat. At least that burn, he could appreciate. There was no doubt each of the newly married couples—Megan and Mark, Arabella and Jay, Wiley and Grace, Kane and Layla and Brady and Harper—were deliriously happy. But Brian had a difficult time sharing in the joy at the moment.

As he gestured to the bartender for another round, his gaze caught on a flash of red out of the corner of his eye. A woman was making her way through the crowd toward the hallway that led to the bathrooms. Her coppery hair, piled high on her head, was a sharp contrast to the creamy expanse of skin revealed by her dress.

Her back was to him, but Brian was immediately fascinated by all that flaming hair, which seemed to sparkle under the lights of the ballroom.

"Is that bow tie cutting off the circulation to your brain?" Josh asked with a nudge.

Brian blinked, then turned his attention to his brother. "More like the unspoken pressure to couple up is suffocating me," he muttered.

"Cheers to that." As the waiter placed another whiskey on the bar in front of Brian, Josh lifted his glass in a toast. Stefan joined them, and all three men drank in companionable silence for a few weighted moments.

"You'd think everyone would be satisfied that three of us have taken the plunge," Brian said as the alcohol heated his veins and the presence of two other confirmed bachelors comforted him a bit. "But Mom seems more determined than ever to marry off all of us. It's like she's a tiger who's gotten a taste for wedded bliss and is on a rampage for more."

Josh chuckled and gestured toward their parents, who danced along with the other couples. Gary and Catherine Fortune had been married for over three decades. While their father still carried a chip on his shoulder from not knowing about his complicated history with the Fortunes until recently, Catherine was most interested in ensuring that her children ended up happy and settled. "A 'rampaging tiger' might be a bit of an exaggeration, Bri. Although your high school English teacher would be impressed with the imagery."

"I feel you with the tiger." Stefan reached around Josh to offer Brian a fist bump of solidarity. He inclined his head toward his brother Mark, one of tonight's grooms. As if on cue, Mark leaned down to kiss his new bride, Brian and Josh's cousin Megan. "The Mendozas have a history of marrying Fortunes. A long history, according to every matchmaking mother I've talked to tonight. I can't help but feel like the freshest meat around."

"With nary a vegetarian in sight," Brian added.

Although Josh rolled his eyes at Brian's lame attempt at humor, Stefan nodded sagely. "Oh, it's definitely hunting season around here." He let out what sounded like a tiny yelp of distress as he watched Belle Fortune, another of the remaining single Fortunes, approach. The gleam in her eye could only be described as predatory.

Hunting season, indeed.

"Well, isn't this a heart-melting trio," Belle said in her sunny way, her gaze lingering on Stefan.

Brian had only met the children of his uncle Miles since arriving in Rambling Rose. The cheerful and pretty blond had relocated from New Orleans, and her sister Savannah was happily married to Stefan's brother Chaz.

"No hearts melting over here," Stefan answered quickly, draining his glass in one nervous swallow.

Belle's grin widened, and Josh subtly elbowed Brian as she took a step closer to the dark-haired Mendoza, who looked a bit like a rabbit cornered by a wolf in a gorgeous satin dress. Tigers… wolves…maybe Brian was mixing up his predators, but he couldn't help but be glad to see the attention focused on Stefan and not him.

A glance around the room made it clear that several of the Mendoza men were watching the interchange, and they seemed as entertained by it as Brian and Josh.

"I know you have a heart, Stefan," Belle practically cooed. She reached out one dainty finger and pressed it to the front of his tuxedo jacket. "Chaz has told me stories about you. You're a big softie on the inside."

"Chaz lies," Stefan managed, his voice unnaturally tight.

It was obvious he didn't want to be outright rude to sweet and flirty Belle but also just as clear he didn't know how to deal with her spirited attention.

Brian's experience as Brady's lifelong wingman kicked in when he recognized the banked panic in Stefan's dark eyes. He rose from his stool and held out a hand to Belle as the music changed to a slow ballad.

"Hey, cousin, may I have this dance?"

Belle narrowed her eyes for a moment as if she could tell what he was up to, but then she smiled and took his hand. "I love to dance." Before turning away, she pointed a finger at Stefan. "Remember that, okay?"

He nodded, then threw a grateful look at Brian, who nearly laughed at Stefan's obvious relief. Even so, he leaned in toward Belle as they made their way to the dance floor. "You know, Stefan was just saying how Mendozas always end up with Fortunes. And the two of you are both single. It's quite a coincidence."

She squeezed his hand. "Trust me. I know."

Bro code was one thing, but it was also damn fun to watch another man squirm.

They talked about the wedding and various members of the extended family as they danced.

"It's amazing to have so many of us together," Belle said. "Although keeping track of all the different wedding gifts coming in has been a full-time job for the brides."

Her comment made Brian remember the horse sculpture stashed in his trunk. He hadn't had time this past week to do any research on its origins, but maybe Belle would know something.

She grimaced as he described the bust and Tyler's reaction to it, but her gaze grew contemplative as he told her about the unsigned card.

"Now that you mention random gifts," she said, "I had a present in my room when I first arrived. It was a framed picture of a rose. At first, I figured it was a wedding favor given to all the guests, but no one else I talked to received it." She shook her head. "I can't imagine the two gifts are related, but they're both antiques and sort of random."

"True," Brian agreed. "Although flower art isn't as likely to strike fear in the hearts of children as a demonic horse head. Who knows? Maybe you've got a secret admirer."

He was surprised she didn't strain a muscle, given how fast her head whipped around so she could glance at Stefan. With a laugh, Brian turned her on the dance floor, only to have his gaze snag on the auburn-hued woman who'd caught his eye earlier.

"I was making a joke about the admirer," he told Belle, pulling his attention away from the captivating stranger. She was standing on the edge of the dance floor, her hands clasped in front of her as she stared straight ahead like she was lost in thought.

Oh, how he wanted to know what she was thinking about. A strange urge for Brian, who'd discovered after his college sweetheart broke his heart that the less he showed he cared about women, the more they seemed to like him. He'd learned a hard lesson about playing his emotions close to the vest and had no reason to think about changing the rule book now.

"But what if I do?" Belle let out a breathless sigh. "Wouldn't that be the most romantic thing ever, especially at this hotel and with the wedding? Love might be in the air for more Fortunes than the ones who got married today."

He refocused on his cousin and couldn't help offering her a warning. "You're clearly going to make some man very lucky, Belle, but be careful about wearing your heart on your sleeve. That's a sure way for someone to rip it off and stomp all over it." He forced the emotion out of his voice, then added, "Trust me."

"There's a person out there for everyone," she said with a conviction that matched his. "I just know it."

His gaze strayed to the beautiful stranger as the music ended, but he pulled his focus back to Belle. "That's a sweet thought, but it's bound to lead to a cavity or two if you let—"

"Even you," she interrupted, poking him in the chest with a laugh. "Maybe this is your year, Brian. But you're going to have to clean up that poopy attitude and be willing to try."

He arched a brow as he followed her from the dance floor. "Did you just use the word *poopy*?"

"You can start trying now." She grabbed his hand and took a sharp turn away from the bar.

"What are you doing?" He slowed his steps, but she only pulled harder, glancing over her shoulder at him with a knowing wink.

A moment later they were standing in front of the flame-haired woman. Her big blue eyes widened in surprise, a look he imagined was mirrored on his own face.

He listened through the dull ringing in his head as Belle introduced herself and him to the stranger, who offered a smile that literally took his breath away.

So much so that he missed getting her name and only realized Belle had asked him a question he also hadn't heard when she elbowed him in the ribs.

"Oof." He cringed at the amused look the

stranger gave him as he desperately tried to put all the working parts of his brain back in order. Maybe those drinks with Josh and Stefan had affected him more than he thought.

"Well, this is fun," Belle said brightly. Too brightly. He might not know his New Orleans cousin well, but right now she reminded him of his sister, meddling and far too smug for her own good.

He shook his head as conflicting desires waged a quick battle inside him. Part of him wanted to lean in closer to the stranger, something about her presence soothing a part of him he hadn't realized was on edge. But another bit told him to run away fast. He didn't understand the intensity of what he felt for a woman he'd just met. He knew for certain it wasn't just the alcohol having its way with him.

The music abruptly ended, and Belle clasped her hands in front of her chest. "It's almost midnight," she announced with a little trill of excitement. "I'm going to go find—" she paused, then took a deep breath "—someone to help me ring in the new year. You two have fun."

Fun.

What the hell was she talking about?

Before he could ask, his bubbly cousin disappeared into the crowd.

Brian let out a soft growl of frustration as he

ran a hand through his hair. Then he glanced at the woman, who looked like she was madly praying for the floor to open up and swallow her whole.

He might not have the charm and charisma of his brother, but he knew enough not to be a jerk by making a beautiful woman uncomfortable.

"Tell me your name again," he said with what he hoped was a friendly smile.

"Emmaline," she said softly, her voice a low purr that reverberated through him. She had a voice that was as gorgeous as her.

"Nice to meet you. I'm Brian."

"Yes." She inclined her head, studying him like maybe he'd just bumped his head. "I know."

Being on the receiving end of her sharp focus made him fidget, and he looked around wildly as Callum Fortune, who'd joined the band on the dais set up at the far side of the room, began to lead the crowd in the countdown to the new year. Callum was the mastermind behind much of the new development in Rambling Rose, and Brian had a huge amount of respect for his successful cousin.

A waiter passed by with a tray of champagne flutes, and Brian grabbed two and handed one to Emmaline, who took it but didn't drink.

He took a long swallow of the fizzy liquid, which did nothing for his equilibrium, and turned to face the party. Why were his nerves going wild right now? He'd been through plenty of New Year's countdowns. He knew the drill. A kiss at the stroke of midnight didn't mean anything. It was tradition. Nothing more.

But as a chorus of claps and bells ringing and shouts of "Happy New Year" filled the ballroom, a funny feeling bubbled up inside of Brian that had nothing to do with the champagne.

Emmaline stood next to him, still as a statue, holding the stem of the glass so tightly he thought it might shatter between her fingers.

He wasn't the awkward teen he'd been years ago, relegated to Brady's shadow. He was a man now. Thirty years old and with too much experience to allow one potential kiss to mess with his head.

"Happy New Year," he said to Emmaline, making sure to bank the emotion pulsing through him. He gave her a practiced smile. The smile that had women back in Buffalo opening their hearts—and their beds—to him without fail.

Color infused Emmaline's cheeks, charming him despite all his self-professed experience. She clinked her glass softly against his. "Happy New Year, Brian."

His name on her lips sounded...right somehow. And it did far more than the alcohol to soothe the maelstrom of nerves inside him. So he did what he was supposed to do at the stroke of midnight when in the company of a beautiful woman. A woman with eyes so clear it felt like he could see an entire expanse of summer sky in their crystal depths.

He leaned in to kiss her.

Emmaline promptly startled, her champagne splashing against his tux as she turned her head. Brian ended up bussing her cheek, then cringing at how badly he'd misread the situation.

Maybe some things never changed.

Was she absolutely the biggest idiot on the planet?

That was the question scurrying around Emmaline's mind like an overcaffeinated squirrel. Brian Fortune, a man so handsome he made her toes curl just by looking at her, had leaned in for a New Year's Eve kiss and she'd messed it up.

Royally.

Like she was the queen of awkward moments.

She felt like a prize fool as she grabbed a discarded napkin from a nearby table to dab at his damp tuxedo jacket. Her face burned, in equal parts from embarrassment and the lingering heat of his mouth on her skin. And, oh heavens, she couldn't help but notice that his chest was hard, obviously muscled, under her touch.

"I'm sorry," she said, keeping her gaze focused

on his bow tie. She could not look him in the eye after how she'd behaved like some nervous schoolgirl.

She couldn't even blame her ridiculous behavior on alcohol. Not that she was a big drinker in the first place, but Emmaline hadn't touched a drop all night. She'd skipped the champagne toast that kicked off the reception and the glass Brian had handed her was now spilled all over him and the floor.

She also hadn't gotten caught up in the moment, because she'd ruined it before there'd even been a chance at a moment.

"You don't have to apologize," he said in that deep voice, and she had to force her knees not to buckle with longing. Why did this man have such an effect on her?

She'd met his twin brother, Brady, along with several of the other Fortune men during her time working at the hotel. All of them had won big in the looks lottery, but Emmaline didn't feel the deep pull of attraction to any man the way she did with Brian.

She blamed hormones, but there was no way she would share that tidbit with him.

"I should be the one to tell you that I'm sorry," he said, covering her hand with his and taking the napkin and then the empty champagne flute from her other hand. He stepped around her to deposit them on a table, and she got an unobstructed view of the reception.

People were dancing and laughing and seeming to enjoy the first minutes of the new year. The volume level of the guests had risen even higher since the countdown, although as Brian returned to his position facing her, all of the noise and revelry seemed to fade away.

If only she could get a do-over on that kiss. Emmaline understood kissing the person closest to her was a New Year's Eve tradition and didn't mean anything. Everyone knew that.

She just had a feeling it would have meant something with Brian Fortune.

"I wanted you to kiss me," she blurted. Another blunder from the queen of awkward moments.

Brian's thick brows rose. She knew he and his twin were supposedly identical. They had the same chestnut-brown hair and dark eyes. But where Brady exuded confidence and easy charm, Brian appeared a bit more reserved. His strong jaw was unyielding and his eyes gave no hint of what he felt inside. He was like an enigma wrapped in a riddle wrapped in a puzzle.

Emmaline had grown up an only child of a single mother who worked long hours. She'd often been left to entertain herself, and she was very good at solving puzzles.

"Because it was midnight on New Year's Eve," she said, cursing the heat she felt rising to her cheeks once again. "Tradition and luck and all that. I kind of reacted without thinking. Too bad this isn't one of those movies where we can rewind the time." Could she actually babble any more?

She clamped shut her mouth and tried for a casual smile to let him know this was all a big joke for her.

Unfortunately, the curse of many redheads, including Emmaline, was that they blushed deep enough to match their hair color. She had very little chance of hiding her embarrassment, because she knew it was written all over her skin.

Brian obviously saw it, based on how his gaze roamed over her face. She expected him to smirk or tease her about it. Most people did. Instead, his eyes darkened to a rich espresso hue. For an instant, he wasn't as much a puzzle as an open book. And what she read in his gaze was desire.

For her.

"I have no control over time," he said, the barest hint of a smile curving one corner of his mouth. "But I've heard a rumor that midnight kisses on New Year's Eve are highly overrated."

Disappointment spiked through Emmaline, but

Brian continued, "However, a kiss in the first few minutes of the new year is a different story."

"It is?" She swallowed and, without thinking about it, licked her lips.

Brian's expression didn't change, but the air between them thickened as he nodded. "It's a fresh start, a new chapter, a world of possibilities."

"I like the sound of that."

"Me, too. May I kiss you, Emmaline?"

Welp. There it was. He was actually asking her permission. As if Emmaline could be more taken with him, his quiet question pushed her over the edge of reason.

She was smitten. The kind of enamored that had her wondering if he might be able to hear her heart pounding against her rib cage. As if her anticipation was a palpable thing.

After a moment, she nodded, not trusting her voice.

Brian's warm hands lifted to her face, and he cupped her cheeks as if she were precious to him. She felt precious.

He leaned in and brushed his lips against hers, featherlight and controlled. Her body erupted in goosebumps and she let out a tiny moan, both in satisfaction and frustration. She reveled in the sensations swirling through her and, at the same time, wanted more.

Brian must have heard the sound—another tally in her list of embarrassments for this night—but he didn't seem to find anything wrong with it.

In fact, it seemed to spur him on. The kiss turned deeper as he shifted both of them into a nearby alcove so she couldn't be seen by the crowd.

He continued to cup her cheeks, the softness of his touch in sharp contrast to the hard planes of the chest she could feel under her hands. But when he lowered one hand to the small of her back to pull her closer, Emmaline wrenched away.

She could not allow herself to be pressed up against him. Not now. Not without revealing… too much.

He looked as dazed as she felt as he stared at her.

"I have to go," she whispered, more to herself than him.

Before he could answer, she turned and ran away.

Chapter Two

"You're staring at that ring like some kind of lovesick schoolgirl," Brian said as he approached the concierge desk of the Hotel Fortune several days later.

Without missing a beat, Brady held up his left hand to more prominently display his new wedding band. Then he picked up a brochure so that his hand wasn't visible to any of the guests milling about the lobby and flipped Brian the bird.

"You're just jealous that you don't have this kind of hardware," he answered.

"Are you kidding? I'd break the hearts of half the women in Buffalo if I settled down."

"Right," Brady agreed with an easy smile. "But take it from me, it's worth it."

"I'll keep that in mind." Although Brian had no intention of settling down. It just wasn't his style. Maybe at one point, he'd thought he would become a family man. Hell, unlike Brady, Brian had dated the same girl all through college. He'd been in love with Tammy. Or he'd thought it was love.

Now the feelings he'd had for his ex had faded so much, he wasn't even sure.

One thing had been certain. She hadn't wanted to spend her life with him. Shortly after they'd both graduated with shiny new undergraduate degrees, he'd come home from work to find her bags packed and sitting in front of the door of the apartment they shared. She'd told him she was moving to Chicago, and when he'd suggested that there were plenty of opportunities for marketing brand managers in the Windy City, she'd cut him off.

Apparently, she'd wanted more excitement in her life and Brian didn't measure up on that count.

Brady stepped out from behind the concierge desk and joined Brian. They were having lunch together before Brady and Harper left on their honeymoon tomorrow.

"How do you feel about Taco Tuesday?" Brady asked as he led the way out of the hotel.

It was a gorgeous January day, with the temperature hovering in the midsixties and a light wind rustling through the holiday decorations that still hung from the windows of most of the storefronts along the town's charming main street.

"I feel good," Brian answered, although he didn't really need to answer. The twins knew each other's tastes and eating preferences without speaking them out loud.

"Let's head over to Provisions," Brady suggested, turning in the direction of the restaurant owned by their triplet cousins, Megan, Ashley and Nicole.

"Do you ever miss the snow?" Brian asked as he drew in a deep breath.

His brother chuckled. "Hell, no. I don't miss driving in it or shoveling it or freezing my butt off most of the winter."

"Yeah, I get that. Do you miss anything about Buffalo?"

Brian knew better than to ask the question. He'd gotten good at pretending he didn't care about being left behind. The more he acted like he didn't care, the more things in life went his way. Women fell all over themselves, and his boss kept giving him more responsibility with the agency's key clients.

He was damn good at his job, creating appealing brands and marketing campaigns for a variety of corporate customers. He chalked up a lot of his success to the time he'd spent observing people throughout his life. Brian was able to read a room or the mood of a crowd without even trying. That ability translated to his work. He could listen to a client's vision for their company, and successfully—and often effortlessly—translate it into a marketing campaign.

The work meant more to him than he let anyone see, and his agency's owner seemed willing to reward him for that with a hefty salary as well as the freedom to work from wherever he wanted and to set his own hours.

Up until this trip to Rambling Rose, he'd had no reason to take advantage of that freedom.

"I wish I could have lunch with you every week." Brady pulled open the heavy wooden door to the restaurant.

"You'd end up fat," Brian said jokingly. When they'd both lived in New York, Brian and Brady had met for lunch once a week at their favorite downtown sports bar to shoot the breeze and catch up on life.

The year since Brady had moved to Texas was the longest they'd ever been apart. "Besides, you're a boring family man. You might cramp my style. The waitresses pay a lot more attention to me now that you're gone."

"Lunch without the winter freeze is even nicer," Brady said as Ashley waved to them from the hostess stand.

"Did you two used to fool people, like in *The Parent Trap*?" Ashley asked with a wide smile. "Nicole, Megan and I used to try to pass for each other, but we're fraternal so we rarely got away with it."

"Except when you study us closer, I'm way more handsome," Brady told her with a wink.

Out of habit, Brian shoved him. "What he's failing to tell you is that I got all the brains."

Ashley laughed at their good-natured ribbing of each other. Brian and Brady had been doing the same routine for years. When they were kids, their mom had stopped dressing them alike because it was too confusing.

The funny thing was they could fool most people, even as adults, but not Harper. When Brian first arrived in Rambling Rose, Brady had wanted to test whether his soon-to-be wife would mistake the two of them.

Brian had come to the hotel, and he and Brady had changed clothes and cars before driving to the house.

The boys had still been at school, so it was just Harper in the kitchen, prepping dinner.

Brian had walked in first, but she'd taken one

look at him and smiled with a shake of her head. "Good try, guys," she'd told them. "But Brady better not get used to driving that fancy sports car. He's going to have too many kids. They'd ruin it in record time."

From that moment, there had been no doubt in Brian's mind that Harper was his brother's soul mate.

They spoke with Ashley for a few more minutes, and after hearing about Brian's recent campaign for a chain of trendy restaurants out of Boston, she'd gently asked if he would mind taking a look at Provisions' website and marketing materials to make possible suggestions for improvement.

Of course Brian agreed and they'd exchanged numbers. He loved talking shop. It was far more comfortable for him than talking about personal matters, and the more time he spent in Rambling Rose, the more he understood the appeal of the small town. He could see so much potential in the way his family was investing in the community.

"Are you ready for a few days off?" he asked his brother after they each ordered the street-taco special of the day.

Brady ran a hand through his hair. "Honestly, I'm not sure if I remember how to take it easy. Toby and Tyler sucked the relaxation out of me real quick."

"It probably goes without saying, but I'm going to say it anyway. You've done amazing with those boys. I had my doubts, but you've really stepped up. Gord would be proud of you."

His brother's features softened at the mention of his late best friend who'd named Brady guardian of his twins. "No one had more doubts than me," he admitted. "But those two numbskulls are the best." He let out a small laugh. "I know we're only going to be gone for a few days, but I'm going to miss them."

"Enjoy the quiet while you can," Brian advised. "Uncle Brian's on the job as twin sitter. Donuts for breakfast every day."

"You'll regret it." Brady pointed a finger at him. "I don't know which is worse with kids. The sugar high or the letdown after."

"You take care of your bride, and I'll take care of your boys." Brian waited until the server had placed their plates on the table and walked away before adding, "I'd tell you to use your honeymoon to get on the baby-making train, but as usual, you're an overachiever in the romance department."

"Only with Harper," Brady countered. "I don't even remember looking at a woman before her."

Brian had just taken a bite of taco, but at Brady's words, that nagging burning in his chest started up again. He swallowed and took a long drink of water. "You've always been lucky."

"Speaking of lucky…" Brady's eyebrows raised. "I heard from an unnamed source that you might have gotten lucky at the stroke of midnight as well. You holding out on me, bro?"

Brian shrugged. He hadn't mentioned the lovely and mysterious Emmaline to anyone. What was he supposed to say? He'd kissed a girl and she'd run away like her house was on fire? Not exactly a testament to his romantic prowess.

Although deep down, he knew his pride wasn't the only reason he'd kept the short interlude to himself.

He could barely think about her without his heart stammering in his chest, and he didn't even know her last name. He certainly wasn't going to talk about it.

"There's nothing to tell," he said casually, plucking up a chip from the plate. "I'm guessing your source is Belle, because she's the one who practically pushed me into a stranger at the reception. That one is too much of romantic for her own good."

"Who was the woman?" Brady asked. "Did you like her? Rambling Rose is a small town. I'm sure someone knows her."

"It doesn't mean anything," Brian said, unsure whether he was trying to convince Brady or himself.

To his great relief, Ashley approached the table to check on whether they were enjoying lunch. Her presence was enough of a distraction to save him from sharing anything about Emmaline with Brady. Yes, he could have figured out who she was with a few inquiries. But why bother?

She obviously hadn't been interested, and he was going to have his hands full with the twins. It was a simple New Year's kiss that would quickly fade into a distant memory.

At least that's what he wanted to believe.

They finished their meal and started back toward the hotel. Brian's BMW was parked in front, and as they got closer, he suddenly remembered the horse sculpture that was still stowed in his trunk.

"While you're on your trip, I'm going to look into who sent that bizarre gift," he told Brady. "Did you ask around at the hotel?"

They'd agreed that Brady would see if any of the Hotel Fortune staff remembered the gift being delivered or knew where it might have come from.

"No leads," his twin told him, then took his wallet out of his pants pocket. "But Grace suggested we contact the owner of this local antique shop."

He handed Brian a card embossed with the

name of the store, Rosebud Antiques. In the corner of the simple card, the words E. Lewis, Proprietor were printed.

"That's the place she got a lot of the decorative pieces for the hotel. Maybe the horse came from there. It's definitely old."

"Old and creepy," Brian agreed. "I'll check it out." He glanced at his watch. "I've got about an hour until my next call, so I'm going to head over now."

"Good idea." Brady clapped him on the shoulder. "Because once Harper and I leave, you aren't going to be in the mental state to manage anything after dealing with the twins."

"They aren't so hard." Brian scoffed. "And I don't scare easily. If you can do it, I can do it better."

"Famous last words," Brady said with a laugh as they parted ways.

Brian grinned and headed toward Rosebud Antiques.

Emmaline heard the bells above the door jingle from where she was crouched on the floor behind the cash register. "Be with you in a minute," she called and reached her arm farther under the counter. A drawer knob had fallen and rolled under it a few minutes earlier.

Unfortunately, she couldn't quite get to it, especially since it wasn't exactly comfortable at the moment to flatten herself onto her belly.

She'd grab a broom later, she told herself as she straightened, dusting off the front of the denim overalls she wore.

Turning to greet the new customer, her breath caught in her throat. Brian Fortune stared at her like he'd just seen a ghost. As his gaze tracked from her face and then down her body, Emmaline resisted the urge to lift her hands to cover her belly.

Although it was unlikely someone she'd met once, despite the kiss they'd shared, would notice she was pregnant. Even six months pregnant, although her baby bump was getting harder to hide.

She was growing tired of concealing it, but she'd made a promise to her mother, who was worried about the gossip that would ensue once word spread through the close-knit community.

Emmaline had already disappointed her mom by returning to Rambling Rose instead of staying in Houston to build a life in the big city, something her mom hadn't had the opportunity to do. She didn't want to add to her mother's discomfort.

"Hello, Emmaline," Brian said as he moved closer. He'd schooled his features from surprise to a casual sort of curiosity she found difficult to believe.

Not when her heart hammered in her chest and her palms had grown sweaty as she remembered how it had felt to have his lips on hers.

"Hi."

She placed her hands on the counter, hoping the cool tile might absorb some of the heat swirling through her. Based on his reaction, she didn't think Brian had come looking for her. She forced herself not to be disappointed by that thought. She'd been the one to run away after all.

He frowned as if he was still trying to make sense of her presence in the shop. "Do you work here?"

"I do. Can I help you with something?" She inclined her head at the packing box he held.

"Um, well…first, it's nice to see you again. I didn't expect… You look…"

She let out a small laugh. "I look like an urchin compared to the night at the wedding reception," she said, feeling like he needed to be let off the hook. "The night we met."

"Overalls suit you," he said, then frowned. "Not that you didn't look beautiful in your fancy dress. But…" He paused, then continued on a rush of breath, "You look even prettier now."

"Oh."

Once again, she wondered how in the world was she supposed to curb her attraction when he shared things like that, looking adorably uncomfortable that he'd said the words out loud? Like he'd revealed something too private.

"Is your boss here?"

Her smile widened. "I am the boss." She didn't try to hide the pride in her voice.

He shifted the box to one arm and pulled a business card out of the pocket of his canvas jacket. She had to admit he looked just as handsome dressed in a casual Henley, dark jeans and the tan jacket as he had in the tuxedo.

So much for convincing herself that her initial reaction had just been the energy of the wedding and the new year.

"E. Lewis," he read from the card she'd had printed a month earlier.

She'd inherited Rosebud Antiques after her grandfather's death last year, but it had taken a while to believe it was truly hers. Working with Grace at the hotel had been what propelled Emmaline to feel like a real business owner.

"Emmaline Lewis," she told Brian.

"Right." He nodded. "I didn't catch your last name at the wedding."

"It's not important," she said, even though it stung the tiniest bit. She was used to being overlooked or not special enough to commit to memory for most people, despite her red hair. Really, that feature was the only remarkable thing about her.

"I was too caught up in the moment with you." He shook his head and flashed a tight smile, like he'd once again said too much.

For Emmaline, Brian seemed to say all the right things.

"I need help with an antique." He placed the box on the counter and opened it.

Emmaline drew closer until the front of her overalls brushed the edge of the counter. Brian pushed aside the tissue paper and pulled out a bronze bust of a horse with the patina of age but in remarkably good shape.

She reached out to touch the tip of the ear at the same time Brian brushed a hand across it. Their fingers connected, and she was somehow unsurprised at the jolt of electricity that went through her.

"This is really something. Where did you get it?" she asked as they both drew back.

"Something," he repeated with a deep chuckle. "That's a politically correct description, Ms. Lewis. My brother and Harper received it as a wedding gift, but it arrived right before Christmas. Harper thought maybe it came from Mariana's Market, but she called out there and they knew nothing about it. There was no card, and to be honest, it scared his boys."

She lifted the sculpture from the box and turned it in her hands. The weight of the piece as well as the craftsmanship of the carvings made her believe it was an authentic antique and not some mass-produced replica.

"You aren't scary," she said to the horse. "You've just been around the block a few times, and it shows. I hope a piece like this wouldn't end up in a flea market, even one as eclectic as Mariana's. Someone with talent made you. Right, sweetheart?"

This was the part of her job that she loved the most. The history of each item and discovering what it would take to find out the origins. Who had originally crafted this sculpture and how could she track down the artist and the era during which it was made? Sometimes the antique business was straightforward, but Emmaline enjoyed the puzzle-solving aspect when she got a chance for that.

Brian cleared his throat. She glanced up with a start, realizing she'd zoned out studying the bust of the horse.

"Do you talk to all your antiques?" he asked with a grin.

She opened her mouth to deny it, then forced herself to tell the truth. "Most of them." She looked around the crowded shop. "Even the furniture. I'm not saying they talk back or I pretend I'm in some animated movie having conversations with bewitched, inanimate objects, but…"

How could she explain without sounding silly? Her ex-boyfriend had outright made fun of her devotion to her grandfather's shop and her love of old things. Robert's opinion had been that if Emmaline had the social skills to make real friends and invest in her future, she wouldn't care so much about spending time focused on items that belonged in the past.

"Go on," Brian urged softly.

She glanced up at him from beneath her lashes, her hold on the base of the sculpture tightening slightly. But instead of condemnation or judgment, his whiskey-hued gaze was filled with curiosity, as if she was making sense and he cared.

"I love the history and the hunt for just the right antiques to sell in the store. The pieces we carry have a story to tell, and it's important to me that I honor that. Most of my customers and clients, like Grace at the hotel, appreciate both the quality of the antiques and the idea of having a tie to what came before." She shook her head. "I probably make it mean more than it does."

"No." Brian covered her hand with his for a brief second, then drew it back like he didn't feel comfortable touching her. "I get what you're saying. I do marketing and branding back in Buffalo, and part of what makes me so good at my job is that I tap into the story our clients want to tell. The history of a company or how they want to be remembered and what their brand means to them and their customers." He blew out a long breath. "I've never said it out loud that way, but it's what I believe. A lot of people think marketing is just about selling products, but it means more to me. Just like the antiques do to you."

A knot of tension loosened inside Emmaline as she smiled up at him. She wouldn't have expected to have something so important to her in common with this man, but it made her inordinately happy that they shared the same sentiment.

"So you're the best at what you do?" she asked lightly before the emotion of the major crush she'd developed on Brian was written all over her face.

"Naturally." He winked. "You probably guessed that, though."

"Of course," she agreed with a laugh. "If the recent changes in Rambling Rose have taught us anything, it's that the Fortunes are a remarkable family. I'd expect the same of you."

His gaze turned contemplative. "I'm not sure about that. I might be remarkable in my job, but I'm the boring one in my branch of the Fortune family."

Emmaline found that hard to believe, based on how fascinating she found him.

"What do you think about the horse?" he asked before she could respond. It was clear he didn't want to go into detail about family dynamics, and she had no right to push him. Or comfort him, although the urge to reach out was hard to resist.

"My grandfather, who started Rosebud Antiques, focused on furniture with European origins, although he also had a great respect for Texas artists. I have a feeling this horse was made by someone in the state." As she drew one finger across the base, she noticed a ridge along the back. "Look at this." She held up the piece so Brian could see what she'd found. "It's some kind of compartment."

"Is there anything in it?" He sounded dubious. "I don't think someone would hide a wedding card like it was some kind of game."

"It's locked." Emmaline studied the compartment for some sort of latch to open it, then glanced toward the door when the bells jingled again.

"Hi, Mr. Truman," she called to the man who'd just entered. "Be with you in a minute." She placed the horse back in the box. "He's one of my best customers," she said, inclining her head toward the older man. "Owns a couple dozen car washes in Houston and is building a second house in the gated community here. I'm helping him furnish it. We have an appointment this afternoon."

"Then, you need to go."

Yes, but Emmaline didn't want to say goodbye to Brian or give up on the mystery of the horse. "Can I keep this for a couple of days?" She gently closed the lid to the box. "I'd like to do some research on its possible origins."

"Sure," Brian agreed, then gave her that hint of a smile again. "It will give me an excuse to see you again."

Her stomach felt light and tumbly. Why did he affect her this way? She was about to tell him he didn't need an excuse, but Mr. Truman cleared his throat with obvious impatience. The man was a great client, but he was also demanding of Emmaline's time.

Brian took a pen from a cup on the counter and wrote a phone number on one corner of the box. "If you need to reach me," he told her. "Otherwise, I'll check back with you."

She nodded and watched as he walked out of the store, understanding that she shouldn't miss a man she barely knew but feeling the ache in her heart just the same.

Chapter Three

"What in the world are you wearing?"

Emmaline forced a smile and stepped back from the entrance of her apartment above the antique shop the following evening.

"Hi, Mom. It's nice to see you. I'm feeling well. How are you?"

Krista Lewis didn't take the hint about good manners. "Put on a sweatshirt, Emmaline. That shirt is…"

"Don't say *indecent*," Emmaline warned, closing the door with a snick and counting to ten in her head. She smoothed a hand over the soft cotton of her T-shirt. "It's a baby bump. I'm not flashing cleavage all over town."

"You didn't have cleavage before this," her mother reminded her.

Emmaline smiled and glanced down at her chest, which was definitely more ample in pregnancy than it had ever been before. She didn't mind the change—any of the changes to her body—because they represented the life growing inside her. A baby girl, she'd found out during her ultrasound. A daughter she already loved with her whole heart.

"I don't want to keep pretending," she told her mom. "It's not as if people aren't going to realize it eventually."

"Trust me," her mother said with a weary sigh. "The longer until word gets out, the better for you."

Emmaline turned away so her mom wouldn't see the hurt she was having trouble hiding. She filled the teakettle that sat on the stove and turned on the burner. She and her mom liked having tea together. It was one of their rituals, and Emmaline hoped it would ease some of the tension between them, at least for a few minutes.

Becoming a single mother might not have been part of her plan, but very little of her life so far had gone according to plan. She was making the best of it anyway, and she was happy. But her mom's constant judgment and regret on Emmaline's behalf definitely cast a pall on that happiness.

"The wedding was gorgeous," she said as she

pulled two mugs from a cabinet. Changing the subject was one of her go-to methods for distracting her mother.

"I still don't understand why you were invited." Krista took a seat at one of the slipcovered chairs at the small antique cherry table. "As if those Fortunes don't have enough people to show off to already. The whole family is too big for their britches if you ask me."

Which Emmaline hadn't, of course.

"I've gotten to know them while I helped with the hotel decor. They're good people, Mom. Kind and down-to-earth, and they've brought a lot of new visitors to town." She held up two tins of tea bags. "Chamomile or peach?"

Krista frowned. "Do you have any apple cinnamon?"

"Not at the moment."

"I suppose peach will be okay, then."

Big or small, one thing Emmaline could count on was her ability to disappoint her mother. She unwrapped the tea bags and placed them in the mugs, waiting for the whistle to sound on the kettle.

"I was just working on month-end numbers." She gestured to the laptop sitting on the table near her mother's right hand. "The shop did a great clip of business in December. It's the fifth straight month with an upward trend. I wish Papa could have seen this."

"Your grandfather never managed that store the way it needed to be. He priced things too low for their value."

"He wanted people to be able to afford to have beautiful things…pieces of history…in their homes. It was his gift to the world."

Her mother sniffed, but whatever she mumbled under her breath was drowned out by the shrill kettle whistle, much to Emmaline's relief. She took comfort in the ritual of pouring the tea, inhaling the warm aroma of peach and allowing the warmth of it to soothe her jumbled nerves.

It wasn't just Krista who was making Emmaline feel out of sorts. She'd been this way since Brian had come into Rosebud yesterday. Ever since their kiss, she'd been distracted by thoughts of the handsome Fortune.

She'd even had a lovely—and quite explicit— dream about him the previous night, which she knew was a recipe for frustration. Emmaline was no naive schoolgirl. The baby currently jabbing a foot into her sternum was proof of that. It would do her no good to spend time fantasizing about things that weren't meant to be.

Placing the tea on the table in front of her mother, she slid into the chair across from her.

"I almost forgot," her mother said, digging into the outsize tote bag that she'd set on the floor. "The reason I stopped over was to give you something I found in your grandfather's things."

When Emmaline had moved back to Rambling Rose, she'd lived with her mother in the small house just outside town, where she'd grown up. It was simple but neat and tidy, and since her pregnancy, she'd had a new appreciation for how hard her mom had worked to create a good life for Emmaline. She wanted to do the same for her baby.

But the friction between them had quickly risen to the surface, as Krista couldn't seem to hold back her thoughts on Emmaline's pregnancy.

It had been easier with her long hours in the shop to move into her grandfather's old apartment, which had been filled with boxes of papers and mementos. She and her mom had divided the contents so they could share in the work of going through everything.

Most of what Emmaline had found were old receipts or articles clipped from newspapers and magazines. But she'd also discovered a stack of letters her grandfather had sent to her grandma, who'd died when Emmaline was a baby. Love letters written during his time overseas in the navy and a precious testament to the love they'd shared.

True love had remained elusive for her mother,

but Emmaline still believed in it. Even if she didn't have time to think about romance with everything going on in her life at the moment.

Someday, her prince would come.

Or she'd find a way to go out and meet him.

Right now, her baby came first. And that meant growing the shop so she could provide for her child. The idea of what she was taking on might weigh down some women, but Emmaline liked it. She was like her grandfather in that she wanted to be rooted. Rosebud Antiques and her life in Rambling Rose were a big part of that.

"I thought you'd like to have it," her mom said as she slid a black-and-white photograph across the table.

The edges were worn and the image slightly faded, but Emmaline could clearly see her grandfather, Albert, standing proudly as a young man under the sign for Rosebud Antiques.

"Look on the back," her mother told her. "It's dated the first day he opened the store."

Emotion clogged Emmaline's throat, and she didn't think pregnancy hormones were to blame. "He looks so happy."

"He was happy in the store," her mother said gently. "Just like you. I know you think I'm being ridiculous, encouraging you to keep your pregnancy a secret."

"There's a fine line," Emmaline said with a soft laugh, "between encouraging and demanding."

"Times may have changed since I was in your shoes," her mother continued as if Emmaline hadn't spoken. "But this town has stayed the same in a lot of ways, despite all the so-called improvements your Fortune friends have brought with them. I loved you from the moment I peed on that stick."

As Emmaline laughed again, her mother reached out and took her hands. "One of the hardest things I've ever had to go through was the cruelty and censure I received because I was an unwed mother. To this day, there are women in town who make a point of flashing their wedding rings in my direction. I don't want that for you."

"It could be different," Emmaline insisted, although she wasn't confident in that statement. If she had been, she would have ignored her mom and proudly shared her news with everyone she knew.

"For some," her mother conceded, "but not all. Your papa died knowing his beloved shop was in your capable hands, Em. Lord knows it's not the future I would have chosen for you, and I'll admit I had plans to take a well-earned vacation with the money we would have gotten from selling this old building."

"I hate that my dream is costing you yours." Emmaline squeezed her mother's hands. Her fingers were long but the knuckles slightly swollen from the years she'd spent cleaning houses and commercial buildings around town. They were hands that told the story of a lifetime of hard work.

"I want you to be happy," her mother said simply. "You and your grandfather shared a love for antiques and this town. This photo reminded me of that. I want you to remember, even when you think I'm harsh, that my intention is pure. Keep watch over yourself and your heart, Emmaline. That's the surest way I know to protect your child as well."

It was difficult to process this sentimentality from her mother. Krista was a pull-up-your-big-girl-panties kind of parent and had left the sweetness to Emmaline's grandfather for most of her life. Albert had been a sunny optimist and a dreamer. His own version of Don Quixote, and Emmaline had loved him for it.

She'd also been aware of what her mother had gone through. There had been girls growing up who talked about Krista like she was less-than because of the hand life had dealt her. Emmaline knew that her mom had tried to find love. She'd had a number of boyfriends over the years, but something had always gotten in the way.

Emmaline, for the most part. When push came

to shove, Krista had never been willing to stay with a man long-term if she didn't think he would also love Emmaline like a daughter.

None of them had, and Emmaline couldn't help but wonder what was lacking in her that no one—not even the man who was her biological dad—wanted to be a true father to her.

Her baby would never feel that sense of lacking or shame. Not if she had anything to do about it.

"I'll remember that, Mom. I appreciate everything you did for me."

Her mother scoffed and pushed away from the table. "You were an easy kid, Em. I can remember so many times when people asked me if you had trouble speaking, because you were so quiet. We'd forget you were in the room."

Had that been it? Emmaline knew her mom made the comment as a joke, but now she thought back to some of the men she'd dated, trying to make conversation with her. It hadn't been that she didn't want to get to know them or have them like her.

She'd just been so nervous about doing or saying the right thing that she'd made it awkward. Just like she had on New Year's Eve with Brian, turning her head when he leaned in for a kiss, then running away like a big scaredy-cat when the kiss they'd finally shared had knocked her socks off.

"Want to have some ice cream and watch *Gil-*

more Girls reruns?" she asked as her mom took a step toward the front door. They'd loved the show back when Emmaline was a kid, and Emmaline had imagined that Rambling Rose could turn into something as charming as the fictional town of Stars Hollow. It had in many ways, thanks to the new life breathed into it by the Fortunes.

She had to believe that would make her hometown a kind and inclusive place to raise her child.

Krista turned slowly and glanced at the small, vintage TV shoved in the corner of the room. "Does that thing even get cable?"

"I have it on DVD," Emmaline told her.

"Yes, I know." Her mother smiled. "I'm the one who bought it for you." She placed her purse on the counter. "What season are you on?"

"Two. Jess just got to town."

"My favorite," her mother murmured. "You get the DVD set up and I'll dish out the ice cream."

Emmaline breathed out a strangely contented breath. Her life might not be perfect, but if she stayed focused on what was important, she could make it into the best life possible for herself and her daughter.

The following evening, Brian ran a hand through his hair and threw a longing glance at the refrigerator in his brother's kitchen on his way to the laundry room. Brady had stocked it with a six-pack of Brian's favorite IPA before driving away with Harper early that morning. He'd claimed that Brian might feel like he needed a beer more than his next breath by the time his four days alone with the twins was over.

It hadn't even taken twenty-four hours for that prediction to come true, although at this point, Brian didn't have the energy to relax and enjoy a drink.

How did Harper and Brady manage those two adorable hellions? How had his mom survived having twins in addition to her other children? Was it some sort of superhuman ability or was Brian just completely incompetent?

"Peanut butter," he muttered as he grabbed a stack of clean towels from the top of the dryer. The twins were waiting for him in the bath, thanks to an incident with chewing gum in Tyler's hair that had somehow resulted in the two of them covered in sticky peanut butter, which they'd tried to use to, "unstick the gum on our own, Uncle Brian." What in the world had they been thinking?

At the moment it didn't matter. He needed to stay on task. A heavy clunk from the floor overhead sent terror shooting through him, and he bolted for the stairs, taking them two at a time.

He could hear Toby and Tyler arguing and burst

into the master bathroom to find both of them standing at the edge of the tub, dripping water all over the tile floor.

The floor was littered with plastic blocks.

"He dropped the spaceship I built, and now it's ruined," Toby accused, giving his brother a not-so-gentle shove.

Tyler lost his footing in the bath and went down, more water sloshing over the side of the tub.

"Toby, you can't push your brother in the bath." Brian hurried forward. "He could hit his head."

"Good," Toby mumbled. "He can break like my ship."

Brian reached into the tub and hauled Tyler up to a sitting position. "You okay?" he asked the quieter twin, who was valiantly trying to control his trembling chin.

Tyler nodded and swiped a hand across his face. Bubbles clung to his thick lashes. "I didn't mean to drop the ship. It slipped."

"We'll rebuild it," Brian told both the boys. "Easier than we could fix one of you if you got hurt." He pointed a finger at Toby. "On your butt. It's dangerous to stand in the bathtub."

"Harper says we have to say *bottom*," Toby reported as he plopped down. "*Butt* is a bad word."

"Seriously?" Brian couldn't fathom that, not

when there were so many other curse words pinging around his brain.

"Toby called me a butt face," Tyler explained.

Even in his frazzled state, Brian felt his lips twitch with the effort to hold back a smile. "That explains it." He pushed aside the broken pieces of the toy and knelt in front of the tub. Despite having rolled up his sleeves, the entire front of his sweatshirt was practically dripping wet.

He'd picked the boys up from school earlier and taken them to a park to throw a ball and play tag. Harper had told him that the more he could wear them out, the easier they'd settle in the evening. She didn't mention the fact that he'd also end up exhausted. Brian was used to long days but not the added responsibility of taking care of children.

When they'd gotten home, Brian had given the boys a snack. Toby and Tyler had spent an hour building some sort of elaborate space station out of construction blocks, a project they'd begun with Brady the previous night. In a moment of supreme stupidity, Brian had inwardly congratulated himself on keeping things under control.

One of the reasons he was so good at his job was his ability to multitask. Maybe when Brady came home, he'd give his twin some tips on managing the household with ease by putting systems and routines in place.

He'd pulled out the lasagna Harper had left in the fridge, at that point deciding to wait until they sat down to eat to pop open a beer in his own honor.

As if in response to his smug confidence, things had gone straight to hell from there. He'd received a frantic call from the agency's owner. Seeing the East Coast was two hours later, Brady had known before even answering that it must be an emergency. Indeed, the CEO of one of their biggest clients—a wellness company that relied heavily on their family-friendly image—had gotten himself embroiled in a scandal of monumental proportions. Brian had spent the next forty-five minutes hashing out strategies for salvaging the brand.

Of course, he'd had the foresight to turn on the television for the boys before taking the call and moving to the front porch for more privacy. He knew Brady and Harper limited screen time, so watching their favorite cartoon before dinner would be a treat and one he figured he could count on to keep them occupied for quite a while.

He'd been so wrong.

By the time he'd come up with a plan, reassuring both his boss and the CEO of the company in question, the lasagna had burned, leaving a charred, smoky mess in the oven. He'd quickly opened the windows and doors, telling himself that if a random smoke alarm was the worst thing that happened, he was still doing okay. Surely there was something in the freezer he could bake.

Then he'd realized that the twins weren't on the couch where he'd left them. And the house had been eerily silent. A bad sort of silence.

Which was when he'd found Toby and Tyler in the bathroom, both of them covered in peanut butter. Head to toe.

The boys had quickly explained that Tyler had gotten chewing gum—which they technically weren't allowed to have—stuck in his hair. Apparently, this wasn't the first time it had happened, so they knew enough to use peanut butter to dislodge the gum. Only that had turned into a bit of a food fight until they were both covered in the sticky, sloppy substance and the room smelled like a nut factory.

So much for his writing a manual on child-rearing.

Currently, they were on their second bath. He'd had to change the water after a first cleaning. It was now almost seven, and no one had eaten dinner, which was probably a contributing factor to their bickering.

How in the world did his brother manage this?

"Lean back," he told Toby, scooping water into the cup. The more outgoing of the twins refused to dunk his head under the water for a rinse. Brian remembered how his mother used to manage the same thing for him when he'd been afraid to get water in his eyes.

He supported the boy's thin back, careful not to let the bathwater drip onto his face. Once both boys were squeaky clean and no longer smelling of roasted nuts, he helped them towel off, then changed into dry clothes himself and went down to scavenge for dinner while they put on their pajamas.

They ate a not-so-healthy but easy dinner of boxed mac and cheese with chopped hot dogs mixed in. After rebuilding the spaceship and reading them several stories, Brian finally closed the door to the twins' bedroom.

The beer sounded appealing, but he still had a couple of hours work to do to get it to his boss by the start of business in New York the following morning. He opened his laptop on the kitchen table, then reached for his phone, hoping he hadn't missed any important calls or messages during project peanut butter clean-up.

His breath caught for a moment at the text from the unfamiliar number. It was Emmaline, messaging him to say she'd discovered a few interesting facts about the sculpture if he wanted to stop by Rosebud or give her a call the following morning. The fact that she'd included an emoji of a horse made him smile for no apparent reason. If this night had gone to hell, at least it was ending on a good note.

Before he could type in a response, he heard a small voice call his name.

Tyler stood at the foot of the stairs, a raggedy stuffed bear clasped tightly in front of him. "I miss them," he said in a shaky voice.

For a moment, Brian wondered if the kid was talking about Brady and Harper or about the parents he'd lost in that tragic accident. The thought of what the twins had been through made his chest ache in a way he knew had nothing to do with heartburn from their makeshift dinner.

"I bet they miss you, too." He flipped closed his laptop and stood. "How about if I lay down with you for a minute? Just until you fall asleep."

The boy nodded and his shoulders visibly relaxed. Work could wait, Brian reminded himself and lifted Tyler into his arms, then headed back upstairs.

Brian had always looked up to his twin. After tonight, one thing he knew for certain was that Brady had been elevated in his opinion to the status of a certified hero.

Chapter Four

Emmaline told herself it didn't matter that she hadn't heard back from Brian after her text.

And if anyone asked, there was no way she'd admit that she'd checked her resolutely silent phone every few minutes until she'd gone to bed and then when she'd woken in the middle of the night to go to the bathroom as well as the moment her alarm went off early this morning.

She hadn't asked him a question or demanded a reply. Heck, for all she knew he'd written down his number wrong and she'd sent the text to some random person who'd deleted it without a second thought.

No sense ruminating over it.

Even though that's exactly what she was doing.

Foot traffic in the shop had been brisk all day and then she'd gotten a call about previewing an estate sale scheduled for the following weekend. She'd made plans to close early tomorrow so she could drive out to the old farm and walk through the house and meet with the family.

The property was nearly an hour outside Rambling Rose, and she felt a keen sense of pride that she'd been called instead of one of the bigger antique stores in Austin.

Everything was going according to plan, she told herself as she nibbled one edge of a cracker. The morning sickness she'd experienced in the first part of her pregnancy had mainly disappeared, but her stomach was still sensitive, and if she didn't eat a little something at regular intervals, the nausea tended to rear up again.

She rang up a purchase of a set of art-deco dishes, packed them for the customer, then turned to set up a display of porcelain china as the woman left the store.

"Hello, Emmaline," a deep voice said from behind her.

So shocked by the familiar tone, she nearly dropped the tureen she held, stumbling over a nearby stool as she tried to make sure it didn't hit the ground.

Likely she would have been the one to hit the ground if Brian's strong arms hadn't caught her.

"Whoa," he murmured into her ear, holding her for a moment longer than necessary before loosening his grip. "I didn't mean to startle you."

"Where'd you come from?" She placed the tureen on the shelf and reflexively tugged on the hem of the baggy sweater she wore. How much longer would she be able to hide her pregnancy?

"New York, originally," he said with a chuckle. "Sorry about that. We walked in as the lady with the dishes was walking out, so the bell didn't jingle."

"We?" she couldn't help but ask, her gaze drawn toward a woman with long, dark hair, standing near the front of the store. Maybe Brian had been too busy to return her text last night.

"Uncle Brian, can I get this slingshot?"

An adorable boy with brown hair and a mischievous glint in his eyes popped out from behind an eighteenth-century secretary. Shortly after Emmaline had taken over the store from her grandfather, she'd set up a small section with racks of vintage-inspired toys so that kids could be occupied while their parents shopped. It was similar to the cozy niche her grandfather had created for Emmaline when she was a girl.

"Are you going to shoot it at your brother?"

"Only if he busts up one of my ships again."

Another child joined the first boy; they were mirror images of each other. "I want one, too, 'cause I'll shoot him right back."

"You'll shoot your eye out," Brian said, then winked at Emmaline.

She laughed, understanding the reference to the classic holiday movie. She and her mom had just watched Ralphie's adventures after opening presents on Christmas morning.

"These slingshots are made for target practice," she told the boys. "Not members of your own family."

They both nodded solemnly, and she felt her smile widen.

The woman she'd thought might be the other half of Brian's "we" left the store with a wave, and something eased in Emmaline's chest.

"Boys, come over here and meet Ms. Lewis," Brian told the duo with a glance toward Emmaline. "I'm taking care of my nephews while Brady and Harper are on their honeymoon."

"That's so nice of you," she murmured.

"No biggie," he said, but he looked a bit frazzled, as if being a single parent for a few days might be more than he'd bargained for.

"I'm Emmaline," she told the boys as they walked forward. "It's nice to meet you."

"I'm Toby," the kid in the red sweatshirt told her. He hitched a thumb at his brother. "That's Tyler."

"Are you having fun with your Uncle Brian?" she asked with a smile.

"We had cookies for breakfast," Toby said, nodding. "And hot dogs."

"I slept through the alarm," Brian explained, pointing a finger at the boys. "We talked about keeping our breakfast of champions on the down low, remember?"

"It was the best breakfast ever," Tyler said. Emmaline appreciated the boy's sweetness and obvious loyalty to his uncle.

The shyer twin couldn't quite make eye contact with her, which made Emmaline's heart melt just a little. She'd been a shy child, so she understood how difficult it could be to meet adults. Spending so much time working in her grandfather's store had helped her with that, which was another reason to be grateful to him.

It also gave her an idea. "Would you two be willing to help me with a job while I talk to your uncle for a few minutes?"

Both boys nodded.

She led them behind the counter and pulled a large box from the shelf. "I have a whole container of these vintage dowels, and I need them sorted by color. It's a big task, so I hope you're up to it." She turned and pointed to a jar on top of the counter. "The funny thing is I keep finding loose change around the shop and I put it in there. If you get the dowels all sorted, then the coins in that jar belong to the two of you as payment."

"We'll do it," Toby said, already digging into the box.

"Yeah," Tyler echoed.

She glanced up to find Brian staring at her with a look of astonishment on his face.

"What?"

"How did you know to do that?" He inclined his head toward the twins, who were enthusiastically pulling dowels of various lengths from the box. "I was scared to death to bring them in here with me, thinking they'd destroy the place in minutes."

"I like kids." As if on cue, her baby gave a soft kick. Emmaline closed her eyes for a brief moment to enjoy the sensation. Would her daughter like helping in the store when she was old enough?

"I grew up in the shop," she answered simply.

"But you're not an overly energetic five-year-old boy. Times two."

"I've seen my share. Did you fit that mold as a kid?" She needed to get back to the reason he was in the shop but couldn't prevent—or didn't want to stop—her curiosity about him.

"Occasionally," he said, looking sheepish. "I was more like Tyler, the strong, silent type, even back when I thought arm farts were the most entertaining thing in the world. Brady was more outgoing and charismatic. Everyone loved him."

Oh. There was something about the way he spoke of his brother that made Emmaline know Brian had always played second fiddle, and even now, it weighed on him.

"I'm sure plenty of people loved you, too," she said, unsure why she felt the need to stick up for him. Brian was clearly a man who could take care of himself.

"Sure," he agreed too easily, then shook his head like he was trying to refocus. "So, you discovered something about the Trojan?"

Emmaline frowned, and he offered a boyish grin. Oh, yeah. She could well imagine falling for a man with that kind of smile.

"The horse sculpture," he clarified. "Brady and I started calling it the Trojan horse and then just Trojan because Tyler gets upset when we even mention the piece. That thing did a number on the kid."

"Good to know." Emmaline looked over her shoulder at the boys, then led Brian to the far side of the worktable behind the counter. The bells over the door chimed and she greeted the older couple who entered, focusing on Brian again when the man told her they were just browsing. "I discovered who the artist is." She handed Brian a few articles she'd printed from the internet. "His name is Alonzo Flynn and he was a well-regarded painter and sculptor, originally raised in West Texas. Most of his pieces featured objects or animals of the West. He had a whole series of horses, and based on what I've discovered, I'd say yours is at least seventy-five years old."

"Is it valuable?" Brian asked as he flipped through the pages.

"Possibly," she said. "Especially given that it's in fairly pristine shape for a piece that old. Flynn died almost twenty years ago, so we can't track him down, and he isn't specifically represented by any particular gallery at the moment. I called a couple of places where he used to show his work as well as a few contacts I have in both Houston and Austin. No one knew anything about your specific Trojan horse or how to trace who might have sent it."

Brian glanced up at her, frustration clear in his dark gaze. "So it's a dead end? I'm pretty much failing at the babysitting part. Now I'm going to have to tell Harper that I not only fed her kids crap for breakfast, but she won't be able to write that blasted thank-you note." He narrowed his eyes. "You know, no one expects a thank-you note these days."

"It's still the right thing to do," Emmaline reminded him. "But I haven't given up." She shifted so that the twins definitely wouldn't be able to see the horse, then lifted the sculpture and tapped on the secret compartment she'd found. "Open it," she told Brian.

His gaze cleared. "You managed to unlock it?" He hitched a finger under one edge of the compartment and tugged it open.

Emmaline tipped the piece toward him until the small key she'd discovered earlier fell out. "That was inside."

Brian picked up the key to study it. "ASB," he said softly, reading the letters etched into the metal. "What's it a key to?"

She shook her head. "Not all of the mysteries about the horse have been solved. I don't know what the key opens. It was wrapped in paper inside the compartment, which is why we didn't hear it rattling. It might not be a huge revelation, but we're making progress. Baby steps."

Brian blew out an obviously frustrated sigh. "I

don't even like babies," he muttered, and her heart seemed to freeze inside her chest. "I'd like to take some big, burly, giant steps with this."

He smiled as he spoke, but Emmaline felt like ice water pumped through her veins. Maybe he was making a joke, but the sentiment seemed serious.

"You must like kids," she said, trying to keep her tone light. "Toby and Tyler obviously adore you."

"They're a lot of fun and definitely tug on the old heartstrings," he admitted, almost reluctantly. "But kids are a lot of work. I imagine babies even more so. And you can't throw a ball to a baby. Or solve a mystery with baby steps."

Right. She reminded herself that this was a hypothetical conversation. He didn't really hate babies, although his comments reminded her of what her mom had said about Emmaline's dad. Her father hadn't wanted to be bogged down with the responsibility of a child. Parenting Emmaline cramped his style, so he'd moved out to California to retain his freedom when she was just a toddler.

He'd apparently gotten his fill of freedom years later when he'd met and married a woman almost fifteen years his junior. Emmaline now had a thirteen-year-old half sister she'd never met and received a Christmas card each year from the step-mom she'd never met, with her father's family in matching sweaters. Right down to their two adorable dogs.

"Babies aren't great at catching balls for a few years," she agreed, nearly placing a hand to her stomach as if she could protect her child from Brian's obvious censure. "Kids grow into it."

"Don't get me wrong." He held up his hands as if he'd somehow caught on to her mood. "My brother is happy with his life, and I'm thrilled for him. We're simply on different paths."

"Okay," she said, unable to muster a decent response when she was trying hard to hold it together. There was no point in being upset. She barely knew Brian. They'd shared a smoking-hot kiss, at least by her standards, but that was all. The fantasies she'd created around him in the past couple of days were just that—silly daydreams.

His words were a good reminder that she needed to keep her feet planted in reality.

"You have business in Austin?"

They both turned as the man who'd come in minutes before with his wife ambled up to the counter. "The missus and I lived there for almost thirty years before we moved farther out to the Hill Country. The city has changed a lot, but it's still the best for live music and great food."

Emmaline blinked, trying to follow the man's

comments. Brian must have looked just as confused because the customer reached out a gnarled hand and tapped it against the key Brian still held. "I worked in finance and recognized the safe deposit box key for Austin Savings Bank." He shrugged. "I just assumed..."

"The key was inside a wedding gift someone in my family received," Brian explained. "We didn't know what it opened."

"Definitely a safe deposit box." The man winked at Emmaline. "Maybe one that holds some secret treasure."

"What kind of treasure?" Toby asked as he sidled forward.

Emmaline glanced over to where the boy stood, his brother a few steps behind him with his wide eyes trained on the horse sculpture. She quickly put it into the box and out of sight.

The man took his wallet out of his back pocket and handed Brian a business card. "If you decide to go treasure hunting, ask for Henry Gilday at the bank and tell him Arthur Blaylock sent you. He'll remember me."

"Thanks," Brian said.

The woman joined her husband, holding a brass lamp in her hands. "We're meeting some friends for a drink at the hotel bar. Any chance you could hold this for me so I can pick it up after we're finished? I'd rather not carry it all over town."

"I'd be happy to." Emmaline took the item.

"Thanks for the information," Brian told Arthur. The older man nodded and led his wife from the store.

Emmaline turned her attention to the twins, understanding that Tyler was fixated on the box that held the sculpture. "How did the sorting go?" she asked, stepping between the boy and his view of the box.

"We got them all done," Toby reported. "There were way more blue ones than yellow."

"Twenty-six," Tyler confirmed, finally raising his gaze to hers. "Twenty-six blue, seven red and fourteen yellow."

"Good to know." Emmaline tapped one finger against her chin. "You two just saved me a lot of work. The jar of coins is yours."

"Or you could trade the coins for a sling shot," Brian suggested. Emmaline bit back a smile at the shocked look on his face, like he couldn't quite believe he'd given the twins that option.

"Yes." Toby pumped his small fist in the air. "I'm gonna get so good at that thing."

"Do we each get one?" Tyler asked, giving his twin some major side-eye. "Or do we have to share?"

"You can each pick one." Emmaline reached

out to ruffle his hair. "As long as it's okay with your uncle."

They both turned their attention to Brian. "I don't know," he said slowly. "A slingshot is a big responsibility. How do I know the two of you can handle it?"

"We can," the boys said in unison.

He continued to study them as if wavering on a decision. Another pang of longing surged through Emmaline. She could tell he was just playing with the boys, and she didn't understand how someone who had such a way with kids wouldn't like them or want them.

And how that meant without a doubt that he couldn't be the man for her.

After a few more seconds of teasing and a promise from the twins that they'd be cautious with aiming if he let them have the slingshots, Brian agreed. He winked at Emmaline—there went the thumping of her heart again—then instructed the boys to thank her for her generosity.

She was shocked when they not only shouted their thanks but came forward and threw their arms around her legs for a hug. Then they bustled off to the children's area and toy display to make their selections.

"I can pay you for the slingshots," Brian said when they were alone again.

"No need," she told him and picked up the key once more. "I'll keep working on details of the sculpture, but you should take this in case you decide to make a trip to Austin. I used to go there a lot on buying trips with my grandpa. It's pretty this time of year."

"Oh, yeah?" There was no mistaking the flirtatious lilt to his tone. "Are you interested in driving down with me?"

"No." The word popped out before she could stop it. Before she could tell him yes, which was what her heart wanted to answer. She could see by the look in his dark eyes that she'd surprised and disappointed him. Brian probably wasn't used to women refusing his invitations.

Because most women weren't in Emmaline's situation.

"Things are bustling at the shop," she explained, the silence between them making her uncomfortable. "My mom covers for me if I can't be here, but she's busy all week."

"I get it," he said, although she knew he didn't understand. He couldn't.

Toby and Tyler returned with their choices. A slingshot shaped like a wolf for Tyler and a bear for Toby.

"Nice picks," Brian said, his voice still tight.

"That bear looks fierce, and you know wolves are my favorite animal."

The serious boy nodded, then turned to Emmaline. "Uncle Brian taught us how to howl last night before bed." Both Toby and Tyler launched into a series of whoops and howls, making Emmaline smile.

"You must be quick learners."

"Uncle Brian is a lone wolf," Tyler continued. "An apple predator."

"Apex," Brian said, closing his eyes for a moment and shaking his head. "An apex predator, but that was supposed to remain between us." He grimaced. "The bro code and all."

"Did you know wolves actually mate for life?" Emmaline raised a brow in his direction. "They aren't all loner animals."

"How about meeting me for coffee tomorrow?" Brian countered on a rush of breath. "It won't take long, I promise. I'd like to thank you for your help, and you can tell me more about the mating habits of wolves."

He looked so unsure of himself, which totally melted Emmaline's heart. The smart thing would be to decline the invitation. The less time she spent with Brian, the better, given the way she couldn't seem to control her response to him.

But it would be the polite thing to do, she told

herself. He was a Fortune and his brother the head concierge at the hotel. She didn't want to get the reputation of being prickly or standoffish. Yes, a simple coffee would be good for her business relationship with the family, although as many rationalizations as her mind came up with, her heart wasn't buying any of them.

She simply wanted to spend more time with him.

"Okay," she agreed. "I could meet you in the morning before I open the shop."

"Perfect." His relieved grin disarmed her. "How does eight thirty work? I'll drop the boys at school and then head over."

"Sure. Eight thirty is perfect."

His grin widened. "It's a date."

The boys thanked her again and they all left the store. When she was alone again, Emmaline placed a hand on her belly to ground herself. A date with Brian Fortune.

Didn't that just sound like the world's biggest temptation?

Chapter Five

Brian parked his car in downtown Rambling Rose the following morning and headed for the coffee shop. He felt slightly more in control today.

At least there hadn't been any peanut-butter catastrophes the previous night. He could thank Emmaline for that. Toby and Tyler had been fascinated with their slingshots. He'd made it clear that they could only shoot wads of crumpled paper in the house. The twins had spent most of the evening setting up rows of green army men on the coffee table then taking turns knocking them down.

He'd promised to take them to a nearby park over the weekend so they could practice with real stones, although he much preferred the paper balls. Brady and Harper had called just before bedtime, and the boys had told them what a great time they were having with their uncle, which satisfied Brian in a way that surprised him.

As he passed the front of the hotel, Grace Fortune, the hotel's manager and his cousin Wiley's new wife, waved to him. She was speaking to a delivery man standing next to a truck with a florist logo on the side. As Brian approached, the man headed to the back of the truck while Grace turned.

"Have you heard from Brady?" she asked. "I hope he's enjoying his mini-honeymoon."

"We talked to them last night," Brian reported. "Both he and Harper sounded totally blissed out."

Grace sighed. "I'm jealous."

"What about you? Do you and Wiley have any romantic getaways planned in the near future?"

"We do, but I'm waiting until we're through the last of the holiday rush. The hotel is keeping me busy but in the best way possible." She motioned to the young delivery guy. "Could you please put the smaller arrangements on the reservation counter and the big one can go on the table in the center of the lobby."

"Gorgeous flowers," Brian murmured.

"We have them brought in fresh each week,"

Grace told him. "It's the little things that make our customers appreciate the hotel."

"I'm actually on my way over to Kirby's Perks. I'm meeting Emmaline Lewis." He had no idea why he felt the need to share that information with Grace, but he was too excited to keep quiet at the moment. "She's helping me track down the origin of the wedding gift Brady and Harper received on Christmas Eve."

"At the coffee shop," Grace said, giving him an assessing stare. "How interesting. So you met after I gave Brady her card?"

"We actually met on New Year's Eve." Brian suddenly felt a bit hot under the collar.

"Belle mentioned you talking to a special lady at the wedding reception. I didn't realize it was Grace. The plot thickens." Grace, who wore a pale pink silk blouse and wide-leg trousers, rubbed her hands together.

"No thickening," Brian said, then cringed at the potential double meaning of his words.

Grace stopped the delivery man on his way in with another arrangement. She plucked several stems out of different sections of the bouquet and then handed the small spray of flowers to Brian. "You can take these to Emmaline."

He took them automatically. "You aren't going to tell Harper about this, right? It's just coffee, and

I don't want my new sister-in-law or Brady going all matchmaker on me."

"My lips are sealed," Grace promised, miming zipping her lips. "Emmaline is a lovely person, Brian. You're a smart man."

"I'm glad you think so," he said with a laugh, then continued on to Kirby's Perks, the trendy coffeehouse a few blocks down from the hotel.

As he entered, all eyes turned to him. He gave a general wave and then quickly made his way to the table in the corner where Emmaline sat.

Today she wore a bulky sweater with a pattern of polka dots across the front of it. Her hair was pulled back into a low knot with two sticks that looked like wooden daggers. A reminder not to get on her bad side, since she wore weapons as hair accessories.

"Why does it feel like everyone is watching me?" He slid into the seat across from her with a glance over his shoulder. People were definitely staring, from the ebony-haired barista to the middle-aged redheaded woman to a bearded old man at a table on the other side of the shop.

"You're new blood," Emmaline said, and it looked like she was trying not to smile. "Plus you're carrying flowers."

"They're for you." He shoved the bouquet in her direction, wondering where the hell the cool and collected man he'd made himself into had gone. He felt as nervous as an inexperienced teen trying to impress his crush and having no idea how to do it. "From Grace."

Emmaline took the blooms from him, her fingers grazing his and sending a current of electricity along his skin. Brian needed to get a hold of himself. It was as if every time he saw her, she appeared more beautiful. Her hair shone like copper in the bright morning light spilling in from the shop's picture window.

He needed to remember to hold on to his composure. Emmaline hadn't exactly seemed thrilled to agree to a date with him, even one as innocuous as coffee. If she knew how much he already liked her, Brian had a feeling he might scare her away.

That was the last thing he wanted.

As she smoothed a hand over the place where he'd bent the stems with his ironclad grasp, Emmaline frowned. "Grace is giving me flowers?"

"She gave them to me to give to you. Because we're on a date."

"We're having coffee," she clarified. "Does that count as a date?"

"I want it to," he said before he lost his nerve. *Stop caring*, he inwardly commanded. Women liked him much better when he didn't care.

Somehow with Emmaline, the emotion wouldn't turn off.

"You probably need some water for those lovely flowers, hon."

Brian tore his gaze away from Emmaline's as a slim woman with clear brown skin and high cheekbones who looked to be in her midthirties approached the table with a small mason jar filled halfway with water.

Color rose to Emmaline's fair cheeks as she smiled at the woman. "Thanks, Kirby," she said as she placed the stems into the glass. "They're from Grace at the hotel."

"Huh." Kirby quirked a brow as she looked between Emmaline and Brian. "So you're just the messenger?"

"Yes." Brian shook his head. "No. I mean, I got the flowers from Grace, but they're from me." He leaned forward and spoke directly to Emmaline. "They are from me."

A small smile played around the corner of her mouth, and he realized she was teasing him.

Better than rejecting him outright, he supposed.

"Kirby, this is Brian Fortune," Emmaline said as she carefully arranged the blooms in the makeshift vase. "He's visiting from New York. Brian, this is Kirby Harris, who makes the best coffee in all of Texas."

"Brady's twin," Kirby said as she gave Emmaline a quick squeeze around the shoulders. "I'm not sure I could tell the two of you apart, to be honest."

"We get that a lot." Brian held out a hand to shake hers. "Nice to meet you."

"Really?" Emmaline raised her gaze to his. "I don't think I could mistake him for you."

"We can't fool Harper," he said. "She's the only one who never fell for our switch-ups. So you'd be in good company. Even our mom sometimes got confused."

Kirby made a hum of approval low in her throat. "Interesting."

"People around here like that word," Brian mumbled, thinking about Grace.

"Well, it's nice to meet you." Kirby turned her attention to Emmaline. "We haven't seen you in here recently, Em."

"Yeah." The blush staining her cheeks darkened. "It's been busy at the shop."

A middle-aged redhead, now wearing a wide smile, joined Kirby. She wore a flowing purple dress with chunky bracelets encircling both of her wrists. "Too busy for your favorite caramel latte and Kirby's famous bran muffins?" She wagged a finger at Emmaline. "Regularity is important, and Kirby's bran muffins will—"

"Rebecca, this is Brian Fortune," Emmaline interrupted. "He's visiting for a few weeks and taking care of the twins while Brady and Harper enjoy their honeymoon." She took the woman's hand, as if by holding on to her she could distract her from more talk of bran and regularity. Brian thought it was adorable.

Kirby stepped forward. "Brian, may I introduce our resident fiction author? I'm honored that she does much of her writing in my shop. She's very talented."

"And regular," Brian said with a smile, unable to help himself. "Nice to meet you, Rebecca."

"I appreciate a man who appreciates the workings of the digestive system," Rebecca told him.

"Enough with the poop talk," an older man called out from a nearby table. "Can't you see the young'uns are on a date?"

"I'm talking about bran muffins, Martin." Rebecca let out a delicate sniff. "Not conjugal relations. Our bodily functions are nothing to be embarrassed about."

Brian's smile broadened when a soft groan escaped Emmaline's lips. She introduced him to Martin and then to the young barista working the counter, who wore head-to-toe black that accentuated her pale skin. Another woman, who Emmaline introduced as Justine and had a baby strapped to the front of her, joined Kirby and Rebecca at the table.

"Morgan is getting so big," Emmaline said as she reached out a hand to stroke the baby's downy hair.

"He only woke twice last night, which is a bit of a miracle at three months." Justine sighed, then leaned her head on Kirby's shoulder for a few seconds. "The promise of Kirby's coffee is the bright spot in my morning. I've missed seeing you around here, Em."

"Busy," Emmaline repeated with a shrug, but something in her tone clued Brian into the fact that there was more to her absence in this shop, where she was clearly a regular, than just work.

She sent him an apologetic smile, but the truth was he didn't mind all of the interruptions. The more time he spent in Rambling Rose, the more he appreciated how close the community was. He'd noticed it with Brady but had chalked that up to his brother's naturally effusive personality and the role he played at the hotel.

Seeing Emmaline with her friends only deepened his appreciation for small-town life. He didn't have these kinds of connection back in upstate New York. Maybe it was his own doing. He tended to stick to the routine of work, the gym and meeting colleagues for drinks or a pick-up game of basketball in the evening. Outside of his job, Brian didn't have a lot of close friends. Brady had always filled that role, but now he was gone.

He drew in a sharp breath as the ache returned to his chest. Funny that he didn't notice it as much when he was with Emmaline.

"We shouldn't keep monopolizing your time," Kirby said, then waved to a couple who entered the coffee shop. "Brian, what can I get started for you? I already know Emmaline's order. Our girl is a creature of habit."

He ordered a large coffee, black, and a bran muffin, earning an enthusiastic nod of approval from Rebecca.

"Actually," Emmaline said before Kirby turned away, "I'll have a decaf latte today and a slice of banana bread. One of my New Year's resolutions is to not be so predictable."

"Decaf," Kirby repeated, her delicate brows drawing together. "That's definitely changing it up for you."

"Wait." Justine's light brown eyes went wide. "Oh, my gosh, Emmaline. I think I know why you're ordering decaf."

"Just concerned about the caffeine jitters," Emmaline said. She smiled as she spoke, but her gaze held a hint of panic.

Undeterred, Justine grabbed Kirby's arm. "I can't believe it. I can, but I can't. I should have guessed it by the way you're glowing. My son is going to have another little friend. And Emmaline will be part of my mom squad."

Rebecca let out a little gasp of excitement.

"What's a mom squad?" Martin asked with a snort.

Brian tried to wrap his brain around what was happening between the women, some sort of speaking in code that he didn't understand.

Emmaline, whose face had turned bright red, darted an apologetic glance in his direction, then looked up at her friends. "You're right," she told Justine. "I'm due this spring."

Brian flinched as a chorus of squealing and congratulations surrounded them. Due for what, he wondered, that would get everyone so excited?

Rebecca reached out a hand toward Emmaline. "May I?" she asked softly.

Emmaline dashed a hand across her cheeks. Was she crying? What the hell was going on?

Then it became suddenly crystal clear as she nodded at her friend. Rebecca placed a hand on Emmaline's stomach and closed her eyes as if in rapture. "Welcome, little one," she said. "You've chosen an amazing mama and we can't wait to meet you when you arrive in the world."

Little one. Arrive in the world.

Brian's gut churned with a kind of manic energy that went far behind the ache in his chest he'd become accustomed to. This felt like flat-out panic.

Emmaline was pregnant.

* * *

Emmaline smiled as her coffee-shop friends gathered around her with hugs and words of congratulations and warm wishes for her baby. Emotion clogged her throat, and relief pounded through her veins.

She'd kept the secret of her pregnancy out of respect for her mom, but she'd started to worry that the friends she'd made in town since her return would pass judgment on her once they knew. Between restoring Rosebud Antiques to its former glory and grieving her grandfather after his death, Emmaline hadn't given herself much time for a real social life.

Her daily visits to Kirby's Perks during long days at the shop had been her one indulgence, and she'd quickly become friends with the other regulars. The fact that she'd stayed away recently had more to do with not wanting to give away her secret. She'd told her mom she wouldn't outright lie about being pregnant, so it had been simpler to keep to herself. As she'd suspected, her friends had realized right away what she was hiding.

Her gaze tracked to Brian, who was staring at her like he was seeing her for the first time. A twinge of regret spiked hard and fast in her gut. She knew she hadn't imagined the attraction between them, and it would have been nice to bask in the glow of his attention for a while longer.

She could have suggested lunch or an easy hike in one of the area parks instead of coffee. But deep down, she understood she'd *wanted* someone to expose her pregnancy. There was no point pretending things could be different with Brian.

After a few minutes of congratulatory conversation, Kirby hustled everyone away from the table with a promise to bring their drinks and food right away.

Emmaline touched a finger to the tip of a yellow blossom and forced a smile. "I bet this is the strangest first date you've ever been on," she said, making her tone light even though sadness weighed heavy in her heart. A silly reaction to losing someone who had never truly been hers to start with.

"I was set up on a blind date once," Brian answered, his hands flat on the table in front of him, "with a woman who'd recently broken up with her long-time boyfriend because he didn't want to get engaged." He frowned. "Then he showed up just as our food arrived and asked her to marry him. Velvet box, down on one knee, the whole bit."

"Seriously?" Emmaline could hardly believe it.

"The woman asked me to take a photo of the two of them with the ring on full display. She left with a fiancé and I went home with her meal in a doggy bag."

"I'm not sure if that makes me feel better or just bad for you."

"It's a good story," Brian said, then sighed. "So is this one."

Kirby returned to the table with two steaming mugs and their baked goods. She also placed a small paper bag in front of Emmaline. "A bran muffin for later. Rebecca insisted."

"Thanks," Emmaline murmured. She took a long sip of the drink and smiled. "I've missed Kirby's coffee."

"Have you really been too busy to stop in?" Brian asked.

"Not really," she admitted. "I was raised by a single mom, and she's worried about how people will treat me, and probably her, once they know about my baby. She asked me to keep the pregnancy under wraps for as long as possible."

"So, you're not married?" Brian asked slowly.

Emmaline covered her mouth with her hand when a laugh-snort escaped. "No."

"And the baby's father…"

"Not in the picture. At all." She leaned in. "Brian, I wouldn't be here with you if I was involved with another man."

His mouth thinned, but he nodded.

Several awkward seconds passed, and Emmaline could imagine Brian mentally planning his escape. That would probably be for the best. It had been quite a blow yesterday when he'd shared his feelings—almost exclusively negative—about kids. Babies in particular.

But she didn't want him to walk away. In addition to being handsome as all get-out, Brian was charming and funny and also a little bit of an outsider, like Emmaline, which only made him more attractive to her.

Of course, she was probably now the opposite of attractive since he knew she was pregnant.

"Warning," she said. "If you leave like that woman on your date, I'm taking your muffin home." She pointed to the plate with the pastry he hadn't taken a bite of yet.

"I can't go," he said, his voice solemn. "Not until I ensure my regularity for the day."

As Emmaline laughed, he unwrapped the muffin, tore off a sizable piece and popped it into his mouth.

"Rebecca means well," Emmaline assured him, taking a small bite of her banana bread.

"Not to belabor the point," Brian said after swallowing, "but I want to be clear. You don't have a boyfriend, correct?"

"Correct."

"Not even on a break or a wisp of a chance of some grand reconciliation?"

"Not a snowball's chance in hell," she confirmed and made an X over her chest. "In fact, we weren't even really together when it happened. I mean, we came together, obviously, but it was a mistake and he wants nothing to do with me or the baby. It's over. Cross my heart."

"Then, pregnancy is for sure not the weirdest thing I've dealt with on a first date."

She smiled, then felt compelled to ask, "You probably won't want a second date, right?"

"I have to admit I got the impression that you weren't interested in me." He ran a hand along his chiseled jaw, and Emmaline's stomach flipped. She wondered if her baby could sense the reaction. "Not to fish for compliments, but the kiss we shared rocked my world. I'd hoped I wasn't the only one to feel something along those lines."

"Oh, I felt something," she said as her cheeks heated. "I also felt bad that you didn't know about the baby," she told him. "It seemed like false advertising."

He chuckled at that. "Just a bit of a shock." He seemed to surprise them both by reaching forward and taking her hand. "I'd like to see you again, Emmaline. I know your life is complicated, and I'm only in town to meet my new niece or nephew. Once Harper has the baby and things settle down, I'll be heading back to New York."

"You can work anywhere," she felt compelled to point out. "You told me that."

"Right." He nodded. "That doesn't change the fact that my life is in Buffalo. I miss having my siblings close, but I spent too much time living in Brady's shadow."

Emmaline wanted to argue. How could Brian think that he had to play a subsidiary role to his brother when he was the most attractive and compelling man she'd ever met?

She didn't say those things, though. He'd told her he wanted to see her again, and revealing how attractive she found him would probably send him running the other way. The fact that her pregnancy hadn't was a miracle.

"I understand," she said, although that wasn't quite the case. "And you're right that things are complicated for me. I'm not looking for anything serious, but I think we could have fun together."

"Lots of fun," he agreed and his voice rumbled along her nerve endings, sending a trail of awareness in their wake.

"We'll keep it casual," she added, more for herself than him. "No promises and no strings attached."

"Casual." He nodded. "I'm great at casual."

Emmaline forced a smile. That made one of them.

Chapter Six

The following morning, Brian knocked on the door to Rosebud Antiques before the shop's scheduled opening and tried to ignore the butterflies dancing across his stomach.

Casual. No strings. No promises.

Those were Emmaline's parameters for dating. At least, dating him over the next few weeks, which worked fine as far as he was concerned, especially since he'd never dated a pregnant woman. He'd never given a pregnant woman another thought other than Harper, and she was having his brother's baby.

Emmaline's pregnancy was a different story,

albeit one he wasn't going to be around to see to the end.

So boundaries made sense and weren't exactly new for Brian. He only dated casually after Tammy had moved on with her life. She'd wanted someone more exciting, she'd told him. Flash and dazzle, which only made Brian think of a cabaret act in Vegas. He wasn't exactly the glitter type.

He also wasn't the type to let someone else take responsibility for his words or actions. There had already been a few missteps with Emmaline. From coming on too strong with that New Year's kiss to showing how out of his element he felt with Toby and Tyler, he hadn't exactly been at his best with her.

When was the last time he'd actually made an effort with a woman? And what did it say about the women he picked that his lack of interest seemed to spur them on even more?

Emmaline wouldn't put up with that nor would he want her to.

Which was why he held up the giant bouquet of flowers he'd picked up for her on his way to town that morning when the door to the shop finally opened.

"Guess who?" he asked. "And for a hint, I'll tell you these flowers aren't from Grace."

His joke was met with a sound somewhere between a sob and a sniff. He quickly lowered the flowers, his heart stammering in his chest as he took in Emmaline's tear-stained face and trembling chin.

"They're just flowers," he said quickly. "If you don't want—"

"The flowers are beautiful." She flashed a watery smile and beckoned him into the shop. "Thank you."

He cringed as she took the bouquet from him, visibly trying to hold herself together. Tears weren't casual as far as Brian was concerned. He did not like to see a woman cry, especially if he couldn't be sure he wasn't the cause of it.

"Let me just put these in water," she told him and turned for the back of the store.

"Are you okay? Is there something I can do, Emmaline?" Brian wasn't certain what possessed him to ask the question. Normally his go-to response to a woman displaying this kind of emotion—any kind of emotion—would be to turn and run the other direction. But with Emmaline, it was different. His heart hurt because she was in some kind of pain.

The ache was different than the one he'd experienced with his brother. Less longing and more wanting to solve whatever was happening. He needed to be careful because this was dangerous territory. At least for a man who only did casual.

He followed her to the shop's cramped office, tethered to her by some sort of invisible string. He watched as she filled the vase with water from the utility sink in the corner. She pulled the blooms out one by one to arrange them just so. Her copper hair was down around her shoulders, and he had to fight the urge to move forward and run his fingers through it. It looked like silken flames, and he had the sudden urge to know if it would be that soft to the touch.

The repetitive motion of arranging the flowers seemed to calm her. The silence between them was comfortable, although Brian had never been a huge talker. He preferred to use his words when they counted and right now he was content to watch Emmaline work. She trimmed a few of the stems with an antique-looking pair of scissors, and he saw her wipe a cheek on the sleeve of her flannel shirt. It still amazed him that as beautiful as he'd found her the night they'd first met, she was even more appealing to him in her everyday clothes.

Today was different, though. Although she wore baggy cargo pants and an oversize shirt, the flannel was unbuttoned to reveal her baby bump in a fitted T-shirt underneath. Now that he knew about her pregnancy, he wasn't sure how he'd ever not guessed. The bump was like a little ball shoved under her shirt.

After another moment she turned to him and it was clear she had her emotions under control. He should be grateful. He should be relieved. Instead, he wanted to know what had upset her and figure out if there was a way he could make it better.

He wanted to be the man who could make it better for her.

"These really are beautiful," she told him. "You didn't have to…"

"I wanted to. I wanted you to know that I don't have to be told what to do by somebody else. I'm my own man."

God, he also wanted to kick himself. He sounded like a total idiot. If he wasn't careful, he would let this woman into his life in a way he hadn't done for many years. In a way that was dangerous to his equilibrium and his heart.

"Tell me what's going on with you. Please." He flashed what he hoped was an endearing smile. "Otherwise I'm going to be left thinking that you burst into tears in response to my flowers. I'd hate to think about what might happen if I brought you a box of chocolates."

She ran a finger over the rim of the glass vase, much like she'd done with the flower petal yesterday. Emmaline might appear reserved, but she was clearly somebody who appreciated physical contact. Brian had never been much of a hand-holder. He didn't like public displays of affection or anything that might give a woman the wrong impression.

Now he reached for Emmaline's hands and linked their fingers together. It felt right, the same way it had when he'd kissed her on New Year's Eve.

"Tell me," he coaxed softly. "I'd like to help if I can."

"It's not you." She kept her gaze fixed on their joined hands. "And I'm not exactly sad. My grand-father, the one who left me this store, died of lung cancer. He'd been a pack-a-day smoker for decades although he'd quit in the last few years. The cancer didn't give him any bonus points for that, unfor-tunately. It was a swift decline, but before things got too bad, he wrote notes to me. Letters about the past and memories he had of our time together in the store."

"He sounds like a good man," Brian murmured.

"He was the best." Emmaline nodded. "I actu-ally went through the shop shortly after his fu-neral because I missed him and I wanted to know what he had to say to me. Before he died, he didn't know he was going to be a great-grandfather. Even though I'm going to be raising my baby as a single mom, I think he would have been happy for me. Family meant the world to him."

"You found another of his letters today?"

"Yes. It had gotten stuck behind a drawer of an old hutch that sold yesterday right before closing. I was cleaning it out before the customer who bought it came to pick it up later. Seeing his writing caught me off guard. I wish he were here." She sniffed and raised her gaze to Brian's. The vulnerability in her sky blue eyes made him want to take a step back, but he held his ground.

She needed him to hold fast in this moment, and he wouldn't let her down.

"Sometimes I wish I wasn't alone," she said.

"I can relate." He ran a hand through his hair and shrugged when she gave him a questioning glance. "It's not like Brady and I were conjoined twins or anything, but he was always around. It's been different back in Buffalo now that I'm the only one of my siblings living there."

"I get that." She squeezed his fingers. "It might be even harder for you because you aren't used to being alone. As an only child, I spent a lot of time by myself, which shouldn't feel that different than now, but it does. I guess we have our loneliness in common as well."

How was it possible that he was taking comfort from her when she had been the one crying minutes earlier?

"You won't be alone for long." He let his gaze drift to her belly, and she quickly pulled her hand away from his and started to button up her shirt. "You don't have to hide from me," he told her. "I like you, Emmaline. Just as you are."

"Then, you need to get your eyesight checked." She laughed self-consciously. "I know how I look when I cry. My eyes get all buggy and red, and my skin becomes splotchy. It's not attractive."

"You're beautiful. No matter what."

Her eyes changed as he said the words. Some of the pain disappeared from them, and he felt a huge amount of satisfaction that he'd been the one to do that. He lifted his hand and used the pad of his thumb to wipe a tear that hung from her bottom lashes.

Tyler had woken from a nightmare last night. According to the boy, the horse from the sculpture had come alive and been chasing him around the school playground. He'd roused his brother, and both boys ended up in bed with Brian. Tyler had snuggled up against him on one side, and Toby'd done his best impression of a starfish on the other. The result was that Brian hadn't gotten near the sleep he needed.

That had to be the reason he was so affected by

Emmaline. Or maybe she was giving off some special pregnancy pheromones. People were always nicer to pregnant women, right? Maybe that had something to do with it.

He couldn't think of another reason and refused to consider that maybe he wasn't quite the lone wolf he'd always prided himself on being. The thought flitted through his brain that possibly he just hadn't found somebody worth changing his ways for, but he blew it away like dandelion fuzz without considering it.

Even though he knew it was a terrible idea—the worst for both of them—he leaned in and kissed her. First, he pressed his lips to the salty tear tracks on each of her cheeks. Then he moved to the corner of her mouth, nipping softly. She rewarded him with a low moan of pleasure and swayed closer.

That's what he wanted. To be as close as he could get to her. Enveloped in her sweet scent and reveling in the soft feel of her skin, it was difficult to remember why this was a bad idea.

They'd agreed to date casually. He kissed women he dated casually. It wasn't a big deal.

What a big fat bucket of lies.

Before things could go too far, he broke away.

She smiled and touch her fingers to her lips as if she wanted to hold his kiss there.

He liked the thought of that.

He liked everything about this woman.

"Come to dinner tonight? I'm staying with my brother while I'm in town." He did his best to keep her from noticing his ragged breathing. "I can't promise anything fancy. And it certainly won't be the most exciting evening. Unless you like Legos and arm farts."

Now her grin widened. "How about if I bring ingredients for a meal? The boys can help set up a taco bar."

"As wonderful as that sounds, it also doesn't seem quite fair. I think if I invite you to dinner, that means I'm supposed to provide it."

She picked up the vase and led him back into the main portion of the shop. "Remember, I'm an independent woman. I own my own business and everything."

Brian wasn't about to admit how intimidating he found her self-sufficiency, which again seemed to say more about him than her. He'd really closed himself off, even more than he'd realized, after his broken engagement.

"Besides…" Emmaline winked at him over her shoulder. "If I bring dinner tonight, that means you'll owe me a different dinner another night."

"Deal," he said without hesitation.

The door to the entrance opened. "Emmaline,

I told you to keep this door locked before business hours."

Brian took an instinctive step away from Emmaline as a woman with her same eyes but not that easy smile moved toward them.

"Mom, we're in Rambling Rose."

"Things are changing around here, missy."

Her mother gave Brian an assessing once-over. "Are you a client?"

He was about to say he was a friend when Emmaline answered, "Yes, this is Brian Fortune. He's the one with the Alonzo Flynn sculpture I was telling you about. Brian, this is my mom, Krista Lewis."

"You're here before the store opens because…?"

"We were just discussing some details about the history of the piece." Emmaline gave Brian a nod that implored him not to contradict her.

"It's nice to meet you, ma'am." Brian might not be the best boyfriend in the world, but he could usually win over mothers with no problem. "Emmaline told me this was your father's shop originally. You have quite the family legacy here."

"Yes, we do," Emmaline's mom agreed, although her tone didn't soften. She glanced at the vase of flowers, and if Brian wasn't mistaken, he would have said her eyes narrowed slightly. "Are you finished meeting?" she asked Emmaline. "I wanted to talk to you before I head for my shift."

"Thanks for stopping by," Emmaline told Brian.

He nodded and headed for the door. So much for winning over the mom. It shouldn't matter. It didn't matter. He and Emmaline were casual because that's what Brian did best.

Chapter Seven

Emmaline parked in front of the tidy two-story brick house later that afternoon, still surprised that Brian had texted with the address and to confirm their date after the way her mom had treated him in the shop.

Once he'd left, Krista had launched into a pointed lecture about focus and priorities. As if Emmaline didn't realize how complicated her life was at the moment and why she didn't have time to fall for a man, especially one who was only in town for a brief time.

Those might be the facts, but they were becoming more difficult to remember by the moment.

Brian surprised her at every turn. The flowers he'd brought her today were lovely, but even more touching was the way he'd handled her breakdown in response to finding the note from her grandfather.

She loved being the proprietress of Rosebud Antiques, but to Emmaline the shop would always belong to Papa. There were even times she'd swear she caught a whiff of Old Spice in the air, the cologne he'd worn for years. As if he were still with her. Albert would have liked Brian. He'd tended to gravitate toward serious people because he'd loved talking about substantive topics, even with customers.

And although Brian could flirt and charm with the best of them, Emmaline sensed an inner solemnity to him that seemed to speak to the essence of who she was inside.

She grabbed the bags of groceries from the trunk and started toward the house. She'd only made it a few steps before the front door opened. Toby and Tyler bounded out and ran toward her, shouting about taco night.

"Uncle Brian says it's gentleman-y for us to carry the stuff," Toby announced as they met her on the walkway.

Emmaline smiled. "That's nice of both of you."

Toby stepped closer. "I'll take the heavier bag 'cause I'm stronger."

"Are not," Tyler argued, reaching for the sack that was clearly the heaviest.

"Am, too." Toby tugged on the bag at the same time Tyler did. Before Emmaline could stop it, the sack fell to the ground. The plastic container of salsa she'd bought at the grocery landed with a thud and burst open. Thick red salsa splattered onto the concrete walk, and both boys gasped in horror.

"Tyler did it," Toby said automatically. "It's his fault."

"Is not." Tyler's voice held the faintest tremble. "You tried to grab it from me, Toby."

Emmaline blinked and looked down at her white sneakers, which were now dotted with splatters of tomato and onion.

She realized there was no time to think about her shoes if she was going to head off a complete meltdown from one or both of the boys. "It was an accident." She placed the second grocery bag onto the lawn and smoothed a hand over Tyler's hair. "We can clean it up."

"I can clean it up," Brian said as he joined their group. "No use crying over spilled salsa." He looked adorably frustrated, but she guessed he was putting on a good face so the boys weren't upset even more.

"Maybe I'll open up a bag of chips and scoop it up that way." He took an exaggerated breath. "Mmm, mmm. There's nothing like the smell of jalapeños and concrete mixed together."

Emmaline laughed right along with Toby and Tyler. How could Brian not want to have kids of his own one day, when he was a natural with them?

"You two can help me hose off the walk while Emmaline takes the rest of the groceries into the house." He gave her a sheepish smile. "Sorry about your shoes. I'll buy you new ones."

"They should clean up in the wash," she said, feeling the butterflies take flight across her middle, a sensation that was becoming all too familiar when she looked at Brian. He wore a SUNY Buffalo sweatshirt and faded jeans that hugged his muscular legs in ways she should probably not notice with two little boys watching.

"I think you just don't want to give up chocolate as your next gift." He winked.

"Who has chocolate?" Toby asked, reaching for the bag on the ground.

Brian picked it up before the boy could and handed the sack to Emmaline. Their fingers grazed, and for a moment, she forgot all about tacos and salsa—and nearly her own name—as a spark of awareness zinged through her.

She headed toward the house before she could do something truly embarrassing, like a full-on swoon. It felt odd to walk into someplace unfamiliar on her own. The interior was cozy with traces of rustic decor in each room. There were photos of Brady and Harper together, several of the boys, and some with all four of them, including a recent one propped up against another frame. It was from the night of the wedding, which seemed like ages ago now. Brady was wearing an identical tux to the one Brian had sported that night. Still, to Emmaline, the twins were easy to tell apart.

Her stomach tightened at the memory of that night and the kiss they'd shared. That led to thoughts of the kiss earlier in the antique shop and how Brian had pulled away before it could turn too heated.

Emmaline shouldn't have been disappointed about that...and yet...

There were several other photos of the boys as babies or toddlers. One of them included a different couple, smiling as they held the twins. Their birth parents, she assumed. Emmaline shifted the bags to one arm as she felt the sudden need to press a hand to her stomach. She was rewarded with a gentle kick from her baby, a physical reminder of the life growing inside her.

Sorrow at what Toby and Tyler had lost threatened to engulf her, and tears pricked the back of her eyes. She understood that her feelings rose to the surface more readily these days and comforted herself in the knowledge that Brady and Harper would give the twins a wonderful life and a happy, loving home.

Who would be there if Emmaline needed someone to rely on? Her mother would help, but in so many ways that counted, Emmaline was truly alone. She shook off her distressing thoughts and headed for the bright and cozy kitchen. There were dishes left in the sink and a plate with a crust of peanut butter toast abandoned on the counter. The little reminders of the fact that two boys lived here made her smile. A Lego figure stood sentry over the abandoned plate and fingerprint smears dotted the stainless steel refrigerator.

This was the life Emmaline wanted. She'd always craved a big family. In her heart of hearts, she had hoped that her mother might find love again and she'd get a younger brother or sister. But it had always just been the two of them along with her grandfather. Eventually she'd made peace with her small family unit.

Was that what would happen with her baby?

She couldn't imagine taking care of the business and a child as well as watching out for her mother and still finding time to date. Except here she was, making dinner for Brian Fortune. The last man she'd expect to find her attractive or to fit so seamlessly into her world.

There was no denying that he did. She'd pre-cooked the meat for the tacos so she searched the cabinets for a pot and set about reheating the shredded chicken as well as the rice and the beans she'd made after closing up the shop a few minutes early.

Not that she exactly believed the adage that the way to a man's heart was through his stomach, but she also had to admit she wanted Brian to enjoy their simple meal. She knew that kids could have the most discerning palates, and she certainly didn't want to end up with a couple of hungry boys on their hands because they wouldn't eat what she'd made.

A few minutes later, Brian and the boys came into the house.

"What the heck happened to the three of you?" she asked with a disbelieving laugh. All three of them were soaked head to foot. Brian shook his head like a wet dog, and she yelped as the cold water sprayed at her.

"That hose had a mind of its own," he told her.

"He sprayed us!" Tyler looked shocked, but his eyes were dancing with glee. "But we got him back even harder."

"Yeah," Toby agreed. "We're the twin team. Nobody can beat us."

Brian enveloped both boys in a bear hug. "Just wait until your dad gets back. We're the original twin team, and I want a rematch. Now, go up and get some dry clothes on, because whatever Miss Emmaline brought for us tonight smells way better than anything I'd serve." The twins dashed for the stairs.

"Is everything a competition with boys?" Emmaline asked.

"Absolutely." Brian took a step toward her, and she couldn't help but notice the way the wet T-shirt hugged the muscular planes of his chest. Her mouth went dry at the strength of his body on display, and she instinctively backed away. It would be so easy to lose control with this man.

"Thank you for being such a good sport about the mess out there." He glanced down at her bare feet and one side of his mouth kicked up. "Cute toes."

Heat rose to her cheeks as she followed his gaze to the alternating pink and purple polish she'd painted on her toes the previous evening. "I'm afraid that in a couple of months I won't be able to reach my toes," she blurted, then covered her face with both hands. "I shouldn't be reminding my date that very soon I'm going to look like I'm smuggling a bowling ball."

Brian gently peeled her hands away from her face and dropped a quick kiss on the tip of her nose. "The sweetest little bowling ball ever." The deep rumble of his voice made a shocking sense of need skitter across her nerve endings.

There was a charged silence between them for a few seconds. Then one of the pots on the stove sizzled, breaking the connection.

She raised a brow. "You're starting to drip on the floor."

He looked down at his feet and frowned. "Harper wouldn't appreciate that." He grabbed a towel out of a drawer and wiped up the mess, then used it on his hair as he headed for the stairs. "I'll be back."

The twins returned before Brian, and she put them to work scooping cheese and sour cream into small bowls. She handled the items from the stove, then took a glance into Harper's pantry. She found canned tomatoes, diced green chilies and a jar of minced garlic.

Grabbing the ingredients, she turned to the boys. "Let's surprise your uncle with some homemade salsa." They cheered and pointed her to where the blender was kept, watching with fascination as the machine whirled the ingredients into a thick puree.

Emmaline opened a bag of chips after dumping the salsa into a bowl and handed one to each of the boys. They scooped up the spicy sauce and munched on their chips, both giving her a thumbs-up.

"No double dipping," Brian called as he entered the room. "Although your mom will be impressed that the salsa is a hit with you both." He came to stand behind the boys, who'd both taken seats at the kitchen island. "You know there are vegetables in salsa. And we all know vegetables are yucky."

"Yucky," the twins shouted in unison.

Emmaline let out a mock, startled gasp. "Don't listen to him," she told Toby and Tyler. She came around the island and hugged Brian around the middle, placing a hand over his mouth. "Vegetables are good and good for you. Trust me."

Brian pulled her closer. "Good advice," he said. "Miss Emmaline is clearly way smarter than me."

She gave him a slow nod and winked. "Because I eat my vegetables."

Since when had the word *vegetable* become sexy? Brian wondered as he looked down into Emmaline's smiling face.

As if she could read the intensity in his gaze, her lips parted, which only made him want to kiss her more. Instead, he released her when she pulled away. The last thing he wanted was the twins reporting to his brother and Harper that they'd seen Uncle Brian kissing the antique-shop owner in the kitchen.

They assembled the tacos, with the boys piling their corn tortillas high. The dinner was filled with lively conversation and, of course, a number of contests between Toby and Tyler.

Who could catch a black bean in his mouth after throwing it the highest? Who could make the biggest crunch with their chip? Who could drink his milk the fastest?

Brian was enjoying a glass of beer, so he didn't partake in the milk challenge but was proud to say that, after an unfortunate incident with a black bean up one nostril, he won at least one contest.

Emmaline laughed right along with the twins and encouraged them in their antics. It made Brian ridiculously happy that she seemed to having a good time on their date.

He wasn't even sure he could call the evening a date but if he did, it was the best one he'd ever had. And Brian considered himself a pretty good date. He knew the best restaurants in Buffalo and had enough pull in town to get a corner table when he requested it. He had friends at the trendiest bars and occasionally drove to New York City for a long weekend with a woman to catch a concert or Broadway show.

But everything in his dating repertoire was by the book. A homemade meal with two rambunctious boys and then a rousing game of Jenga before bedtime wasn't exactly his idea of an exciting night.

So why was this the happiest he'd felt in ages? Maybe it was just relief that with Emmaline's help he'd made it through a successful night with the twins.

Based on the little Emmaline had told him about the man who was her ex-boyfriend and father of her baby, the guy had been a real tool. What kind of man would let his pregnant girlfriend walk away? Particularly when the woman in question was as amazing as Emmaline.

Not that Brian was looking for dad duty in any way, but if he'd been in that guy's situation, he hoped he would have stepped up to the plate. His brother had done exactly that when the twins needed a guardian. At the time, Brian hadn't been able to understand how Brady could change his life on a dime.

Now he understood that the twins had been as much of a blessing for Brady as he had been for them.

Brian wasn't like his brother, though. He'd never been the commanding type or the kind of guy who could easily make friends and adapt to whatever came his way.

At least, he'd never thought of himself that way.

What was it about Emmaline that made him want to become something different? Someone better, at least for his short time in Rambling Rose. He couldn't—or wouldn't—offer her more than that.

The twins insisted that she be part of their bedtime-reading ritual. She seemed happy to oblige and sat on the rocking chair in the corner while Brian read them their favorite adventure story.

Both boys immediately began to complain when he read in his normal voice. He'd become their favorite bedtime reader during his visit because of the different voices he did for each of the characters. It had been one thing when he was on his own or it was just Brady walking past the room to overhear him.

Emmaline wouldn't exactly deem his old lady voice sexy-times material. Would she?

He felt his face heat as he launched into the different characters. There was no point in denying Toby and Tyler. It would just push bedtime out even further.

Both boys were nodding off by the time he finished the story. He tucked them in and finally turned to meet Emmaline's gaze.

He might have expected her to laugh at him, but she looked as charmed as the twins had been.

"That was amazing," she whispered. "They're lucky to have you, Brian."

The words made him feel like he'd just won an Olympic gold medal in the best-ever uncle event.

He took her hand and led her down the stairs. At the bottom, he turned, ready to pull her close and kiss her senseless, the way he'd wanted to most of the night.

Only for Emmaline's mouth to stretch into a wide yawn. She tugged her hand away and pressed it to her cheek. "I'm sorry," she said. "I…" She yawned again. "Oh, gosh. I can't seem to stop."

He smiled and tucked a loose strand of hair behind her ear. "Looks like the twins aren't the only ones ready for bed."

She shook her head. "I wanted to have more time with you. I had a great time tonight, Brian."

"The same can't be said for your shoes."

"They'll be fine."

"Brady and Harper get back the day after tomorrow," Brian told her. "I'd like to take you out on a proper date then."

"Okay." Color bloomed in her cheeks. "That

would be nice." He leaned in, but she held up a finger. "You should know that since Kirby and the gang outed my pregnancy at the coffee shop, I'm not going to hide it anymore." She pressed a hand to her belly. "I'm wearing a baggy shirt tonight because it seemed easier than fielding questions from the boys, but if we go out, there will be questions. And comments."

"I don't care about what anyone else thinks," he assured her and then kissed her gently. "This is about you and me."

Those must have been the right words, because Emmaline wound her arms around his neck and drew closer. "I'm glad," she said, but before he could kiss her again, she yawned once more.

"I'll walk you to your car."

She mock pouted but didn't argue. "I'm definitely not as fun as I used to be," she told him as he picked up the bags with the leftover supplies to carry for her. "Actually I'm not sure I was ever that fun."

"As far as I'm concerned, you're the best."

After another lingering kiss, Emmaline climbed into her car and drove away. Brian watched her taillights until they disappeared around a bend. The night sky overhead was once again filled with stars, and he breathed in the fresh Texas air. He needed to stay in the moment and remember his reason for being in town and how long he planned to stay. He knew better than to examine the feeling of contentment coursing through him. Contentment was fleeting.

One thing he knew for certain was that it couldn't last. He didn't do commitment or let his heart lead the way, no matter how attractive he found her. Her life was going in a very different direction than his and nothing would change that.

Chapter Eight

The following afternoon, Emmaline approached Kirby's Perks with nerves jingling inside her just like the bells above the coffeehouse's front door. She'd thought about coming to the neighboring shop all day, but it had taken longer than she'd expected to gather her courage.

It was silly. Kirby, her staff and the regular customers were Emmaline's friends. Heck, they already knew about her pregnancy. So why was wearing a shirt that showed her rounding belly so difficult?

She realized it was her mother's voice she'd been hearing inside her head over the past several hours. Worrying about whether people would judge her for her situation. Would her friends suddenly decide she was some kind of old-school fallen woman? Maybe that wasn't so appalling, but she understood that subtle judgment could be just as devastating.

Emmaline gave herself a mental head shake and commanded the voice inside her brain to quiet, even if it was her mother's. She loved this baby and had already spent too much time and energy worrying about what other people would think. Her pregnancy might not be by the book or the situation she would have chosen, but she was going to be a good mother. Starting now. No one would make her or her child feel like they deserved less. She'd done that often enough over the past few years.

She made herself small because that's how her ex-boyfriend had wanted it. In a myriad of tiny ways she made compromises—from masking her opinion if she disagreed with him to letting him choose restaurants and activities to trying to convince herself the scraps of affection he gave her were all she deserved. But he was gone and there was no point in allowing the past to taint her future.

She opened the door to the coffee shop and walked in with her head held high. Immediately

Rebecca, who was at her usual table in the corner typing away on her laptop, stood and came forward to wrap Emmaline in a tight hug.

"You look beautiful," the older woman told her. "Positively radiant. I wish we had known earlier, but I'm so happy to share in your joy now. I hope you'll let me be an honorary auntie."

Emmaline drew in a shaky breath. "Of course," she said. "Eventually this little one is going to need somebody to introduce her to all the best literature and edit a term paper or two. We'll be depending on you, Rebecca."

The woman beamed. "I had to drive down to Houston yesterday and stopped in my favorite used bookstore. I might have bought a few children's classics. I just couldn't help myself. I didn't want to be presumptuous, but if you're okay with it, I'll drop them off tomorrow?"

"Thank you," Emmaline whispered. "I've already started reading to my belly at night, so I'd love any books you're willing to share."

"Reading to your belly?" Martin called from a nearby table. "What the heck is that about?"

Rebecca patted Emmaline's shoulder. "You know, Martin, the research says that babies can hear inside the womb. Emmaline is starting this child off on the right track."

Martin let out a snort. "Well, if that's the case,

then I'm gonna bring you some of my old Louis L'Amour books. Might as well get the kid started on the right path for a native Texan."

Emmaline laughed and approached the older man's table as Rebecca returned to her laptop. "Speaking of Texans, I was wondering if you've heard of the artist Alonzo Flynn?"

Martin seemed surprised by the question. Nevertheless he launched right into the artist's bio. "He was a painter and sculptor who worked mostly in bronze and copper. Pretty famous in certain regions of the state."

"Right," Emmaline agreed. "I'm working with a client to learn more about one of his sculptures. We've hit a couple of dead ends, but I'm not giving up."

"That a girl," Martin said quietly. "What's so special about this sculpture?"

Emmaline shrugged. "I'm not really sure yet, but it came with a fairly cryptic message. Brady and Harper received it as a wedding gift, but Brian is helping them track down the gift giver."

"Brian Fortune? Interesting." Martin scratched his beard. "Well, I don't know if I can be of any help, Em. But you'd make your grandpa proud trying to do what you can."

Emmaline's heart had filled with gratitude at Rebecca's generosity and sweet words about the baby. Now it felt like it might burst open. She wanted nothing more than to make her grandfather proud. She also knew that Martin didn't give compliments easily. She squeezed his shoulder, then approached the counter.

The barista waved at her. "Your usual, but decaf?" Annette asked. Her black-rimmed eyes appeared huge underneath all the makeup she wore. As always, she was dressed all in black.

"Please," Emmaline answered. "Would you add a carrot muffin to the order? I need to make sure the baby gets some vegetables."

Annette chuckled. "Did you know there's a whole series of baby albums where they turned rock songs into lullabies? I have a copy of the Metallica one, if you want it. I heard you talking about reading to the baby. My best friend's sister just had her baby. She told me music is good, too."

Emmaline dabbed a finger at the corner of her eye when tears sprang forward. She really did have the best friends ever. It made her sad to think that her mother hadn't gotten this kind of support from the community when she'd been single and pregnant, and she hoped her mom would now appreciate that Emmaline didn't have to hide.

As full as her heart felt, she thought about Brian as she took a seat at the table they'd occupied during their date. She should be content with the blessings she had and not wish for more. Her mom didn't need to tell her that wanting more only led to heartbreak. Emmaline had seen that lesson in action more times than she cared to admit.

Especially for a single mother.

She wasn't sure when her mother had given up on love, but she understood the decision had come after far too many broken hearts. Emmaline had a full life. Now she had Brian for a few weeks of fun, which should be more than enough to satisfy her.

Somehow she knew that wasn't going to be the case.

Brian walked into Roja, where he was meeting his cousin Belle, who was staying at the hotel during her time in Rambling Rose. He slid into the chair across from her as she picked up a pad of paper and shoved it into her overlarge purse. "What are you doing?" he asked.

"Nothing," she muttered. "How are you, Brian? I don't see any permanent scarring from being responsible for the twins for the past few days."

"We've all managed to survive, although I'll be grateful to see Brady and Harper." He checked his watch. "They're due back any minute. Brady said Harper wanted to be home to pick up the boys from school."

"School." Belle's smile turned wistful. "I loved

school. I could have stayed there all day. Most afternoons, I volunteered for my teachers just so I wouldn't have to leave."

He felt his mouth drop open, looking at his blond, vivacious cousin. "You don't look like the type who would have loved school."

Her big blue eyes narrowed. "That's a stereotype about blondes," she told him. "And not a fair one."

He held up his hands. "You're right. I'm sorry. If it makes you feel any better, I hated school."

"Give me a math problem." Belle crossed her arms over her floral-print silk shirt and stared at him.

"You mean like two plus four?" Brian wasn't sure where she was going with this.

"Something hard. An algebra equation. Or calculus. I loved calculus."

"I'm not sure I even know any calculus equations," he admitted. "Wait." He picked up the phone that he'd set on the table and did a quick internet search for an algebraic equation. He rattled it off to Belle, and only seconds later, she answered. The right answer. "How did you do that?"

"It's a gift." Her shoulders relaxed slightly. "People don't expect it of me. I'm smart."

"You might be a genius."

She winked. "Well, thank you. But I'm not the

only Fortune who's smart. Grace told me she saw you on the way to meet Emmaline Lewis. She's the one I introduced you to on New Year's Eve."

"True enough."

Nicole, who ran the hotel's signature restaurant during her time in town, delivered two plates of chicken piccata to their table. "It's the lunch special today," she told them. "A culinary masterpiece, if I do say so myself."

"It looks fantastic," Brian told her. "Thank you. There are a lot of perks to being a Fortune in this town."

Nicole nodded. "That's true, which is why you should consider staying longer. Brady told me you're able to work remotely."

"Yes, but my life is back in Buffalo."

Nicole flashed him a sage smile. "We've all had lives in other places. Rambling Rose is home. You just wait and see."

He shook his head. "That's fine for the rest of you, but I'm good on my own."

Belle leaned in and mock whispered to his cousin, "He fancies himself a lone wolf."

"I didn't say that," Brian argued, even though the teasing made him smile. This was as bad as being ganged up on by his siblings. "I have a comfort level with my routine back in New York."

Nicole glanced at Belle with a knowing look. "He's a stodgy, set-in-his-ways lone wolf."

"I'm going to a restaurant not owned by a family member next time," Brian muttered.

"You say that now. Wait until you take a bite." Nicole lifted her brows as if an invitation.

Brian scooped up a bite of chicken in lemon sauce, along with a juicy caper. As soon as the food hit his mouth, there was an explosion of flavor. "This is really good," he said after he'd swallowed. "It might even be worth all the grief."

"Enjoy," Nicole told them then left when someone called her name from the kitchen.

"Tell me more about this budding romance," Belle urged. "Is it serious between the two of you?"

Brian opened his mouth to answer. Of course it wasn't serious. He'd met Emmaline only two weeks earlier and gone on a couple of casual dates. But it felt serious. It felt different than anything he'd experienced before. And that scared the hell out of him.

So he shook his head. "I'm going back to Buffalo after Harper has the baby," he reminded his cousin. "There's no point in letting things get serious."

"Sometimes you can't control it." Belle took a dainty bite, and Brian could tell she was lost in thought. "Sometimes things are just meant to be."

"Tell me you're not still hung up on Stefan." As Brian took a long drink of water, he recalled his cousin flirting with the Mendoza brother at the weddings. "I warned you about being too free with how you give your heart away."

Belle sighed. "I know, and it was good advice. But there's just something between the Mendozas and Fortunes. Even you have to admit it."

"That doesn't mean there's something between you and Stefan. You can't force something that isn't meant to be."

"What about when it is meant to be?" Belle asked softly. "I still believe there's someone out there for everyone. Maybe I was the person who introduced you to your someone."

Brian's heart shifted at those words. It was like a piece of a puzzle falling into place. That was impossible. For one thing, he didn't do love. For another, in the grand scheme of things he barely knew Emmaline. He was getting caught up in all the happily-ever-afters surrounding him but knew better than to believe he could be part of one.

"Emmaline is pregnant," he said suddenly. That would clearly show his cousin she was barking up the wrong tree with this whole "meant to be" business.

Belle's eyes widened. "How do you know?" She leaned forward. "You only met her on New Year's right? How could you even...?"

"She's six months pregnant," Brian clarified. "She was pregnant when we met."

"She has a boyfriend? A husband?"

"Neither. The boyfriend didn't want anything to do with a baby."

"I hate him already," Belle said, sounding incensed on Emmaline's behalf.

Brian appreciated that streak of loyalty in his cousin. He hoped Emmaline was surrounded by people like that in her life. He wanted to be one of those people, despite the fact that it was only temporary.

"I'm not a big fan of the guy either. At least he's not in her life now."

"But you are."

"Stop trying to make this more than it is," he warned.

Belle tapped her fork on the edge of the plate. "I don't think I am. You two make a cute couple. And her baby is only going to be a couple of months younger than Harper and Brady's baby. They could grow up as best friends. Almost like they were cousins. In every way that counts, they would be cousins."

Brian swallowed as the bite of chicken he'd taken threatened to lodge in his throat. "Whoa, there."

His cousin's words shocked him because he had no intention of sticking around and it terrified him to think that Emmaline might expect more of him than he was willing to give. He'd never planned to be a family man. That was way more Brady's style than Brian's.

He liked his life the way it was. He'd crafted it so that things were simple and easy. He could do what he want when he wanted. If the past few days had taught him anything, it was that kids changed everything. Maybe Brady had a point when he told Brian that the change was for the better.

"You have to admit I might be right," Belle said.

"I don't have to admit anything," Brian countered. But he didn't argue the way he would have before his time with the twins.

He felt a little hot under the collar as Belle studied him like she knew exactly what he was thinking. So he placed his palms on the table, sat up a little straighter and howled. Not loud enough to draw attention from the other diners in the restaurant, but he had the intended consequence of making Belle laugh.

He needed to distract her. He needed to distract himself.

They chatted for a few more minutes about her life back in New Orleans and how much she already loved Rambling Rose. He could tell this town was casting its spell on her, and it was easy to keep her talking. Anything to draw the attention away from himself.

When lunch was over, they parted ways, and he headed out so he could get in a few hours of work before the boys were finished with school. As he started across the lobby of the hotel, he heard his name called in a voice as familiar to him as his own. Brady was at the reservation desk, talking to the young woman behind the counter. He came forward and gripped Brian in a quick hug.

"I owe you, brother. That was just the break Harper and I needed to recharge and get ready for our new addition."

Brian shrugged. "No big deal. Toby and Tyler couldn't beat me, despite their best efforts. I know too many of the twin trade secrets."

"Those two do their best to come up with new material," Brady said with a laugh. "I can't believe how much we missed them. Even only being an hour away and luxuriating in the idea of not having any responsibilities for a short time, it was almost too quiet. Harper is in full-blown nesting mode now, so it's good to be back."

"It's good to have you back." Brian left out the part where he was going to miss having the boys to himself.

"You're not leaving town, right?" Brady's eyes went wide with alarm, a change Brian didn't like. He preferred his brother happy and relaxed, and he liked knowing he'd had something to do with that.

"No, why?"

"I thought maybe the twins would have scared you off. I know how much you like having no responsibilities."

"I have responsibilities back in Buffalo." Brady's casual tone grated under Brian's nerves like a pebble in his shoe he couldn't shake out.

"To your job," Brady agreed. "But not to people. Tammy did a number on you."

"It's a good thing you're back then. I'd hate to screw things up with Toby and Tyler, due to my irresponsible ways, or be a bad influence on them."

Brady's brows drew together. The thing about being a twin was that Brian knew his brother's facial expressions almost as well as he knew his own. He could tell that Brady was irritated by his snippy tone, but Brian was irritated, too.

He had no one to blame but himself. After all, a few minutes ago he'd lifted his face to howl, for heaven's sake. Until coming to Rambling Rose, he'd convinced himself that he was happy with his life. But when Brady pointed it out, somehow Brian came up lacking. It was nothing new, but he wondered if all this time he had been playing second fiddle to his twin because he hadn't had the guts to step into the first chair.

Chapter Nine

Emmaline nearly jumped out of her skin later that night when the doorbell rang. Of course she was expecting Brian. He'd texted earlier and invited her to dinner with just the two of them, now that Brady and Harper had returned.

But she was nervous. Coffee at Kirby's Perks had been one thing. How much could really happen in a crowded coffee shop filled with her friends? Or at a dinner with two five-year-old boys? But tonight would be different.

It was just her and Brian. Her heart fluttered at the thought of spending time alone with him. Of what she wanted their relationship to be, even if it wasn't the best idea for either of them.

She opened the door, and the fluttering in her heart picked up the pace at the sight of Brian sporting a crisp button-down shirt and dark jeans that hugged his muscular legs. He had on a leather bomber jacket, and Emmaline wanted nothing more at that moment than to lean in and take a deep inhale. Which would make him think she was a total weirdo. She had already gotten familiar with his scent, some sort of spicy soap mixed with minty gum. And maybe it was the years spent in her grandfather's shop, but Emmaline loved the smell of leather.

His mouth kicked up at one corner, and she realized she was gaping at him.

"Hi," she breathed.

"Hi." How was it possible to infuse one word with so much meaning? He handed her a box wrapped in gold paper. "I brought these for you. They're small-batch chocolates from a candy store in the Hill Country. The hotel gift shop stocks them, and Grace told me they're really popular with guests. Not that she picked them out. The chocolates are from me, not Grace. So we're clear." He massaged his hand over the back of his neck. "I'm babbling."

"It's fine," Emmaline told him. It was actually a comfort to realize she wasn't the only one nervous about tonight. "Thank you for the chocolates."

"You look amazing."

She stepped back to let him into the apartment. Tonight she'd chosen a dark green A-line dress that had been one of her favorites even before her pregnancy. Some of her clothes no longer fit, but the flowing dress still worked. She knew she'd need to buy maternity clothes soon, or at least, she wanted to. Before Brian it had seemed plausible to get through her pregnancy with baggy sweatpants and oversize shirts. Maybe she was being silly, but she wanted to look pretty for him. And for herself. She wanted to remember that it was okay to be proud of her body and the life she was carrying inside of it.

Her mom had not been happy about her daughter's pregnancy being revealed to the town. But Emmaline enjoyed the attention. Her friends supported her, and if she received a sidelong glance or snarky remark from someone she didn't know well, that was okay. She was okay.

Better than all right, with this handsome man standing in her apartment.

"So…this was your grandpa's old place?"

Emily nodded. "I love being downtown and living above the store. It makes me feel connected to him even though he's gone."

"That's good." He smiled, but she noticed it didn't reach his eyes. "Although sometimes I could use a little less family connection."

"What's going on?" She reached out and placed a hand on his arm, the leather butter soft under her palm.

"Nothing I want to talk about tonight," he said, lifting her hand and pressing a lingering kiss to her knuckles.

Sparks skittered along her skin, but she also felt the slightest twinge of disappointment. Brian's expression was guarded, almost as if he'd lowered a mask of the handsome, charming date he thought a woman would want and expect him to be.

Maybe that would work for most women, but Emmaline liked the real Brian. She wanted to know the things he wouldn't share with other people, like why having a close-knit family might sometimes feel like a burden. Emmaline had always wanted siblings.

"How about a tour?" he asked, his voice low and rumbly.

"Sure." She felt lightheaded when he looked at her that way, like her head was filled with bubbles. "We can start with the bedroom." She let out a squeak of embarrassment when his eyes went wide. "I didn't mean that like it sounded. The apartment isn't large." She tugged her hand away from his grasp and waved it toward the combination kitchen and living room. "Other than the two bedrooms, this is pretty much all of it."

"Trust me, Emmaline, I wasn't complaining." He reached out a finger and touched it to her chin until she looked up at him. "I also didn't take the comment as an invitation. There's no rush for things to move forward between us."

Tell that to her body, Emmaline thought. She nodded. "Of course. I know that." Pregnancy might not have dampened her ability to be attracted to a man, but she couldn't imagine a scenario where Brian would want to be with her.

She led him through the small apartment to the back hall where two bedrooms and one shared bathroom were situated.

"Believe it or not," she said, pointing into the bathroom, "I helped install the tile when I was not much older than Toby and Tyler. The pipes weren't well insulated and they froze one winter when there was an unseasonable cold snap. The bathroom and the part of the store below it flooded. My mom worked a lot, so I spent most afternoons and a lot of weekends with my grandpa. Not just in the store but up in this apartment."

She watched Brian take in the black-and-white subway tile. There was a framed photo of Emmaline as a girl hanging above the towel rack, and he poked his head in to get a better look at it. "You were a cute kid."

"I was a carrottop back then," she said with

a self-deprecating laugh. "Luckily my hair darkened some."

"Your hair is incredible," he told her and suddenly the masked charmer was gone. She could see the intensity in his dark eyes, and an answering yearning bloomed inside her that nearly knocked her over with its force. She quickly headed down the hall again, needing a bit of distance to retain her equilibrium.

"That's my bedroom." She waved a hand toward the master, which really wasn't much bigger than the second bedroom. She didn't even pause in the doorway, worried that if she glanced from her bed to Brian, she might do something foolish like plaster herself against him.

"This is the room that I used to stay in. It will be the nursery."

She flipped on the light for the bedroom at the end of the hall, sighing as she walked in. "I need to get going on projects for the baby. I've been so busy with the store, which is incredible, but I'm going to eventually run out of time."

Brian followed her into the room and moved toward the paint cans she had stacked in one corner. "Are you planning on doing everything yourself?"

"Don't worry. I bought VOC-free paint. And I'm going to open the window to vent the room. My mom has already lectured me, so…"

He held up a hand. "I'm not lecturing." He inclined his head toward the ladder. "Think of it as friendly concern."

Emmaline should appreciate that concern and not let her hackles rise. "I'm a single mom," she said as if that wasn't obvious. "I need to get used to doing things on my own." She rubbed a hand over the cardboard box that held the crib she'd ordered. She'd gotten it for a great deal at a year-end sale, but it was some-assembly-required, and she had yet to start that process.

"I can help."

She blinked, convinced she hadn't heard Brian correctly. "You don't want to help me paint a baby's room and put together furniture. No one wants to put together Scandinavian furniture. It's a great deal, but you definitely pay for the thick instruction booklet."

He grinned. "Put me to work, Em. Now that Brady and Harper are back, I'll have some free time."

"Okay, then. If you want to spend your free time putting together furniture, I'm not going to say no. I might be independent, but I'm not stupid." She grinned. "You must be really looking forward to getting back to your life in Buffalo if this is your idea of a good time in Rambling Rose. This town must be even slower than I thought."

"I don't mind slow," he told her, his voice pitched low. Although he was clearly flirting, Emmaline heard something in his tone that he wasn't saying out loud. There was more to Brian than the polished, slightly reserved, charming-when-he-wanted-to-be city guy. And she was determined to discover all of his secrets.

She grabbed her coat and they walked a few blocks to Provisions, the restaurant owned by the Fortune triplets, where Brian had made a reservation.

"I've wanted to try this place since I moved back to town." Emmaline realized how small her life had become. Her mom was the only person she saw after hours. Most of her friends in the coffee shop were who she considered work friends. Or casual acquaintances. Emmaline wondered how much of that was because people had better things to do than hang out with her or if that was just a story she told herself.

She'd opened herself up to her ex-boyfriend, and that had gotten her nowhere. She gave herself a mental head shake. There was no point in thinking about her loser ex while she was on a date with Brian.

Ashley Fortune Mendoza greeted them at the hostess stand, taking both of Emmaline's hands in hers before congratulating her on her pregnancy and welcoming her to the restaurant.

Emmaline felt a familiar flush rise to her cheeks. She'd never imagined a world where she would be treated as a peer of someone in the illustrious Fortune family. Yes, all of the Fortunes involved in the hotel were nice to her. Most of her work was with Grace, who was also a Rambling Rose native. That made it less intimidating, plus the hotel was one of her best clients.

This felt different. This felt like she belonged because of the man standing next to her.

As if he could sense the change in her, Brian placed an arm around her shoulder. "This is Emmaline's first time at Provisions," he told his cousin. "No pressure." He winked. "But I'm expecting you to help me dazzle her."

"There's no need to dazzle me," Emmaline said. How was she supposed to explain that the very sight of him overwhelmed her?

Ashley's grin widened. "Dazzling is our specialty." She led them through the crowded restaurant to a table in a small alcove that clearly was one of the prime locations in the dining room. "If it's okay with the two of you," Ashley told them, "I'd love to have our chef prepare a special tasting menu. Six courses, and I promise every one will be even better than the last."

"You don't have to…" Emmaline began.

"That sounds perfect," Brian told Ashley. "And we'll start with a bottle of your finest sparkling water."

"Of course," Ashley agreed. She glanced at Emmaline. "Are there any ingredients you don't like or any particular requests?"

"Anything is fine," Emmaline said. In all honesty, she wouldn't even know how to order at a fancy restaurant. Not specifically anyway.

Her ex-boyfriend liked to go out to eat but mostly at sports bars with rows and rows of televisions on the wall and loaded potato skins on the menu. There was nothing wrong with a good potato skin, but Emmaline had a feeling that Provisions was going to ruin her for normal restaurant experiences.

At least she'd have this night to remember when Brian was gone. The thought dimmed a little of her excitement.

"Are you okay?" he asked as if he could read her mood. "Am I coming on too strong? It's been a while since I've tried to impress a woman with a fancy dinner."

Her heart warmed at the flash of vulnerability in his dark eyes.

"You don't need to impress me," she told him.

"I want to," he said softly. "You deserve to be impressed."

Well, if that didn't just send her heart into overdrive.

"You're doing a great job of it, but don't feel like you can't drink on my account. I wasn't much of a drinker even before the pregnancy. But I must admit, in the morning I definitely miss my giant cup of coffee."

"It's all good," Brian assured her. "Although now I've outed us with my family. If I know Ashley, she's already on the phone with Nicole, and they're probably texting Megan at the same time. Be prepared for a flood of Fortunes at the antique shop tomorrow. I just hope Brady isn't one of them. The last thing I need is my brother sticking his nose in my business."

Emmaline reached out and covered his hand with hers. "I think it's sweet that your family is so close."

Brian rolled his eyes. "They all think they know what's best for me."

"And what is that?" she couldn't help but ask.

"Not the life I have back in Buffalo."

"But you like your life." A part of her hoped he would argue with her or say that Rambling Rose was growing on him enough that he might consider staying.

It was a silly thought. Even if he did stay, her life was going to change so much once the baby came. She had to keep reminding herself that this was a man who'd admitted that he didn't even like kids that much. Brian was perfect for a temporary fling, to make her feel special, but there could never be anything more than that.

"I do like my life," he said finally.

Disappointment spiked inside her chest. It was the answer she expected, just not the one she wanted.

A waiter arrived at the table with a large bottle of some fancy sparkling water along with their first course of spiced crab cakes. Brian raised a toast to new beginnings, and Emmaline told herself that she would focus on this beginning instead of concentrating on the ending that was bound to come.

Maybe Emmaline had gotten too used to living in her head. All of that time spent alone in the shop between customers. She daydreamed about the future and rehashed her past, with a tendency to swirl around the drain of second-guessing herself, like she was water emptying from a bathtub.

Brian gave her a reason to stay in the moment. Because every moment with him felt better than anything she could have imagined in her own mind.

They enjoyed a leisurely dinner, talking about

their childhoods and preferences for everything from ice cream flavors to books to favorite movies. It was hard to contain her surprise when he revealed *The Princess Bride* as his top film.

"I pegged you as more a *Terminator* guy," she told him with a laugh. "Not so much as you wish."

He scoffed. "Don't forget the rodents of unusual size from the movie. Yes, there's some romance, but at its heart, that movie is an action-adventure. I'd put Andre the Giant up against Arnold any day of the week."

She laughed some more and then listened as he did the worst Inigo Montoya impression she'd ever heard.

He was laughing, too, and time flew by. As Ashley had promised, the food was amazing. Emmaline could barely eat another bite by the time dessert was brought to the table. Except the dessert was crème brûlèe, which happened to be her favorite.

When Brian spooned up a bite and held it to her mouth, all thoughts of laughter disappeared. She was on a romantic date with a man who, in just a couple of hours, made her happier than she'd felt in years.

She had a hard time staying in the moment when all she could think about was not wanting the moment to end.

He paid the bill, and they left the restaurant. Darkness had fully fallen over the town, but the streetlamps lit the way back toward the shop and her apartment.

"Do you want to watch a movie?" She blurted the question as they approached her door. "If you have to get home, I understand, but—"

"I'd love to," he said as he lifted his hand to the back of her neck. He pulled her close and leaned in for a lingering kiss.

Chapter Ten

Brian couldn't quite understand the nerves he felt as he made himself comfortable on Emmaline's couch. She returned from the bathroom and grabbed the remote from the coffee table before joining him.

"What are you in the mood for?" She looked up at him with those big blue eyes from underneath her long lashes and the only word he could think of was *you*.

Of course he didn't say that. He could tell she was even more nervous than him, and he was determined to be a gentleman. Was there really something special about her? If he'd made more of an effort with the other women he'd dated since his broken engagement, would he have had just as much fun?

He'd gotten used to not trying. There was no way he was going to risk having his heart broken again, and his dates seemed to like him better with a nonchalant attitude.

It had become so easy to not care, but with Emmaline, it was the exact opposite. He didn't think he could stop himself from caring for her if he tried.

"My vote is for *The Princess Bride*," he said.

"As you wish," she murmured, and his heart stuttered.

He'd actually never told anybody about his love for the classic movie. Not that there was necessarily anything to be embarrassed about, but Emmaline had been right. People seemed to peg him as an action-adventure guy. It wasn't that he didn't like those types of movies, but if he was truly being honest, *The Notebook* would top *Rambo* in his mind any day.

Brady would have given him all kinds of grief. Brian wasn't sure when he felt the need to start hiding aspects of his personality that didn't fit with the way his family or friends or coworkers saw him. It was refreshing to be with Emmaline and not feel like he had to hide anything.

As the movie started, he pulled her closer, nestling her into the crook of his arm. She fit perfectly, which was no surprise.

He could tell she was holding herself still, and he also felt when she finally relaxed into him. It had been years since he'd watched this movie and even longer since he'd enjoyed a quiet night at home with a woman. He couldn't imagine any place he'd rather be.

As Brian blinked awake, he watched the movie credits roll. He started to sit up but then heard the sound of Emmaline softly snoring next to him. Her arm was draped across his waist as she slept peacefully on his chest. He felt like he never wanted to move again and disturb her.

She must have sensed a change in him, because she suddenly startled awake, wiping a hand across her chin.

"You snore and drool," he told her, tucking a stray strand of hair behind her ear. "It's adorable."

She rolled her eyes. "It's rude of you to point that out," she grumbled.

He leaned in and pressed a kiss to her forehead. "But I said it was adorable."

"Still rude."

"I talk in my sleep," he offered. "Does that make you feel better?"

"Actually it does a little." She shifted closer. "Thank you," she said against his mouth.

He hoped she didn't expect him to resist her being so close. There was no possible way that could happen. He cupped her face between his hands and kissed her. He savored her sweet taste, and his body seemed to ignite when a soft moan escaped her lips.

He deepened the kiss. She opened for him without question and within moments he was lost in the taste and feel of her.

He jerked away before he completely lost control. "I should go. I don't want to go," he clarified, "but I should go."

"You don't have to go," she told him. She bit down on her lower lip, and he nearly groaned. "You could stay the night. I don't mean that… I don't think I'm ready… I guess I just mean you could sleep here." She covered her eyes with her hand. "That sounds so stupid. I know we're adults. There's nothing stopping us from—"

"I'd love to stay." He interlaced their fingers. "Nothing needs to happen, Em. I wasn't joking when I said I don't mind taking things slow. The idea of holding you all night is the best thing I've ever heard."

She stood and tugged him to follow her. "Best thing I've heard, too," she said as she led him to her bedroom. Her bed had about a dozen pillows and a soft white comforter covering it. It looked infinitely appealing.

"I'm going to, um, brush my teeth and put on my pajamas and..." She looked down at the floor.

"Emmaline, if this is too much, I don't have to stay."

"I want you to," she said without hesitation. "I also don't want you to end up disappointed because this isn't the kind of night you're used to or I can't give you what you expect."

"I don't expect anything," he told her honestly. "I can just hold you." That answer seemed to satisfy her, and her shoulders, which she'd held rigid, relaxed slightly.

"Then, I'll be right back."

She disappeared out of the room, and Brian pressed the heels of his hands to his forehead. *Do not mess this up*, he inwardly commanded. *Remember that it's temporary. Remember that it's casual.*

His heart wasn't paying a damn bit of attention to his head.

He got undressed down to his boxer shorts and climbed into the queen bed. He could tell which side she preferred because the nightstand was piled high with books. He felt as green as a teenage boy waiting for his first love, which was ridiculous. He was an experienced man who'd had plenty of girlfriends. A confirmed bachelor.

The women he'd dated in the past couple of years would have laughed their heads off if they could see him now. Brian wasn't laughing. He was too busy thinking about sleeping next to Emmaline. Of course he wanted her. But he'd been telling the truth when he said he wanted to be close to her as well. It had been a long time since he'd allowed himself to be close to anyone.

It seemed like forever until she returned, although in reality, he knew it hadn't been more than a few minutes. She wore the most adorable pair of polka-dot pajama pants with a matching top. He'd be a liar if he didn't admit his first thought was unfastening those big pink buttons. Instead, he gave her a smile he hoped was encouraging.

"You look comfy."

She grimaced. "That sounds like the opposite of sexy. I guess I wasn't trying for sexy, but…"

"I thought you were sexy when you were snoring," he said, earning another eye roll.

"We shall not speak of my snoring again." She climbed into bed next to him. "I guess it's a pregnancy thing. I never did it before."

Pregnancy. Right. He wasn't just spending the night with a woman he cared about more than he probably should. Her unborn baby was part of the mix. Panic suddenly pricked Brian's chest.

Ever-observant Emmaline propped herself up on one elbow and turned to him. "What's wrong?"

"What if I flail an arm and hit your stomach?"

She let out a little snort of laughter that she tried to cover with a cough.

"You aren't going to hurt me, Brian." Her gaze wandered to his chest, and the smile disappeared from her lips as her eyes went a bit hazy. "I'm more worried about my self-control."

That got his interest.

He tugged the sheet a bit lower. "I'm fairly irresistible, huh?" He made the words a joke, but she nodded solemnly.

"Totally irresistible," she agreed.

"I feel the same about you," he said. He leaned closer, then paused when she let out a giant yawn. "It's probably a good thing for both of us that you're actually tired." He covered his mouth when a yawn escaped his lips as well. "I guess we both are."

He drew her closer. When she was tucked into him, he dropped a kiss on the top of her head. "Go to sleep, Em."

She settled against him and then Brian sucked in a breath when he felt a soft thump against his hip.

"Was that…?"

"Yep," she confirmed. "The baby is usually active right before I go to bed. She'll settle down after a few minutes."

A sense of wonder raced through Brian. Emmaline reached up and turned off the lamp next to the bed. In the quiet of the room, with the only illumination coming from the streetlights filtering through the curtains, the moment felt particularly intimate.

"May I put a hand there?" he asked before he thought better of it. "I don't want to overstep."

She lifted his hand and placed it on her stomach and pressed. His touch was answered with a little kick.

"She likes the attention."

"You know for sure you're having a girl?"

"Yep. I thought about being surprised with the sex when the baby was born, but I figured I'll have enough to deal with. I'm glad I did, because it feels like I'm getting to know her even more this way."

"Hey, little one," Brian said quietly. "It's time for bed."

"Normally I read to her. Rebecca from the coffee shop sent over some more books, and Annette gave me a compilation of rock songs turned into lullabies. They seem to calm her. Help her know she can settle."

"I went through a stage of night terrors," Brian confided, unsure why he was sharing that tidbit of information. He'd known Emmaline for a couple of weeks, but she knew more about him than anyone other than his twin. "My mom would sing me back to sleep. Mostly John Denver songs."

She was silent for a long moment, and he thought maybe he'd revealed too much. Did a woman really want to think of the guy she was dating as a scared kid with nightmares? "Would you sing to her?" she asked finally, her voice barely above a whisper.

The baby kicked again.

"It might be the best way to ensure I get some rest tonight," Emmaline said around another yawn.

He started the first line of "Take Me Home, Country Roads," which had always been his favorite song. A grown man who liked a fairytale movie and John Denver. No wonder he'd had more luck with the ladies when he kept things casual and didn't offer up many details about his own personality. But it felt like a privilege to be asked by Emmaline to sing to her daughter.

He spread his fingers over her belly, amazed each time he felt a soft flutter or kick.

"You have a nice voice," Emmaline said sleepily, and he imagined he felt the same amount of pride in her compliment as a musician winning a Grammy Award.

Brian continued to sing and his whole body relaxed into the moment. He'd hated the nightmares that plagued him as a child, but a part of him had loved those quiet moments alone with his mother.

As one of six children and a twin on top of that, he didn't get much one-on-one time with her. His dad wasn't big on demonstrative displays of affection and had encouraged his wife not to coddle the kids, so those moments had made him feel special. He wanted to make Emmaline feel special.

As he ended the song, he glanced down at her, ready to ask for her next request, only to find that she had fallen asleep. He lay there in the dark for several minutes, listening to her breathing.

The baby had grown quiet as well, but somehow Brian could still sense the unborn child's presence. It felt strange to think that he could have a connection to Emmaline's daughter now, but he wouldn't even know her when she was born.

Surely he'd come back to visit Rambling Rose at some point, so they might run into each other. By that time, Emmaline might be in a new relationship. The idea of that was enough to ruin his peaceful mood, so he put it aside. He wrapped his arm more fully around her, closed his eyes and drifted off to sleep.

A week later, as Emmaline was tidying up Rosebud Antiques, she still couldn't get over the changes in her life. She'd gone from feeling isolated because no one knew about her pregnancy to being surrounded by people who were excited for the next chapter in her life.

Even her mother had seemed to relax a bit, although Emmaline still avoided talking with her about her relationship with Brian. She couldn't explain how close she felt to him when they'd only met on New Year's Eve. Yet there was no denying it.

Since the night of their date at Provisions, she had seen him regularly. Almost every day, although he hadn't stayed the night again. As if by unspoken agreement, she walked him to the door each evening after a prolonged goodbye that involved lots of kissing. Emmaline imagined she wouldn't ever like kissing anyone as much as she did Brian.

It was as if he knew exactly how to make her crazy with need. That was precisely the reason she couldn't have him stay over again. She'd woken that morning in his arms, her body humming with awareness. A subtle shift of her leg had revealed that he was feeling the same way, and oh, how she wanted to act on those feelings.

But Brian had jumped out of bed like his pants were literally on fire, grabbed his clothes and rushed for her bathroom. He'd emerged only a minute or so later fully dressed and then hurried from her apartment after a quick kiss. She'd been shocked and maybe a little disappointed until she'd received a text from him an hour later telling her that he'd had the best night of his life, but that his desire for her was so intense, he didn't trust himself to stick around.

Emmaline had never inspired that kind of desire in anyone. Certainly not her ex-boyfriend. So the fact that a man like Brian Fortune wanted her in that way did a lot to mollify her hurt feelings.

It also surprised her how well he fit into her life. She'd made it a New Year's resolution to increase the internet presence of the shop, so during these winter months she'd decided to close early a couple of days each week and compile online inventory.

Brian joined her at Kirby's Perks, where they shared a table as each of them worked on their own projects. Because most of his clients were on the East Coast, she knew he started work early each morning, so by the afternoon, he was mostly finished with his phone calls and able to assist her.

He had a great eye for design and photographic composition, helping her take pictures of some of the items she wanted to feature on the website and Rosebud's social media accounts. He seemed to enjoy those quiet moments with her in the antique shop and Kirby's Perks as much as she did. It was such a departure from other men she'd dated in the past. Each of her boyfriends—not that there had been many—had made her feel like she wasn't quite enough on her own. Her personality naturally skewed to introverted, so she'd always done her best to make herself seem more interesting or cater to however the guy wanted her to act.

She'd made a vow to herself and her unborn baby that she wasn't going to compromise any longer. She would not raise a daughter who had to watch her mom play small or change for a man. Emmaline wanted her girl to know that she was enough, and the best way to do that would be to model that behavior. So the fact that Brian seemed to like Emmaline for herself came as a revelation.

It also made it more difficult every day to remember that their relationship was temporary and that New Year's was quite possibly the only holiday she'd get to spend with him. Based on Harper's due date and the timeline Brian had explained to her, he'd likely be gone by Valentine's Day. Not that Emmaline had necessarily planned on having a valentine, but the idea of missing Brian made her heart ache.

She glanced up from a shelf she was dusting and smiled as Toby and Tyler ran toward her. Brian gave an apologetic wave as he followed the two boys.

"Mommy's at the doctor," Toby told her, "So Uncle Brian picked us up from school."

Tyler edged in front of his brother. "We asked him to bring us here, so we could show you how good we've gotten with our slingshots."

"I can hit a pop can off the fence from a lot of feet away," Toby boasted.

"I can do it from even more feet." Tyler grinned. "I'm patienter with my aim."

"You're stupider, too," Toby said and gave his twin a hard shove.

"Enough." Brian's voice had an edge to it Emmaline hadn't heard before.

"*Stupider* isn't a word," Tyler muttered as he righted himself.

Toby pushed him again. This time Tyler's shoe caught on the corner of a nearby table, knocking a ceramic pitcher to the ground. It hit the floor and shattered into tiny pieces.

"You broke it," Toby said, his voice hushed, while Tyler burst into silent tears.

"What did I tell you boys?" Brian shouted. "You've got to take care. This isn't the playground." He lifted first Toby and then Tyler away from the broken glass. "What do you say to Miss Emmaline?" he demanded.

"Sorry," Tyler told her.

"Sorry," Toby echoed.

"Accidents happen," she answered both boys. "That's what my grandfather always said. I just got in a new train set in the toy section. Why don't you two go check it out while Uncle Brian and I clean up? Then we can head to the park and you can show me your slingshot skills."

The boys stared at her.

"What's wrong?" she asked.

"Do you hate us now?" Toby asked. "Because we're bad."

"You're not bad, and I don't hate you." She opened her arms and both boys rushed in for a hug. She raised a brow in Brian's direction, and he shrugged.

She grabbed each boy's hand and led them to the toy section before returning to the front of the store. Brian had already grabbed the broom from the back office and was sweeping pieces of the pitcher into a pile.

"What's going on?" she asked at the same time he said, "I'm sorry."

"I wasn't joking, Brian. It was an accident. They happen."

"I shouldn't have brought them here again." She could see how tightly he was gripping the broom handle, and it made her chest ache. "This is my fault."

"Accidents by definition don't assign blame."

He shook his head. "I had a meeting go south this morning, and I haven't recovered since. Then

I forgot Brady had asked me to babysit while he and Harper went to the doctor, so I had to reschedule a conference call with my boss. The boys have been fighting since I picked them up from school and now—"

"Hey." She covered his hand with hers and leaned in to press a soft kiss to his cheek. "I'm glad to see you under any circumstances."

"You can't possibly mean that," he said on a harsh laugh.

"I do, and I'm happy to see the boys."

"You're going to make a great mom, Em."

As glad as she was for the compliment, there was something in his tone that gave her pause. "Tell me what's going on, Brian."

"Do you ever feel like you're messing up every part of your life?"

"All the time."

"Why do I find that hard to believe? You always seem like you have everything under control."

"Then, I'm fooling you," she said with a laugh.

"My brother has it all together, too." Brian gave a small shake of his head. "It's like I'm one step behind right now. Maybe that's why it's smarter for me to keep my life simple. Because I can't handle anything more."

Emmaline wasn't sure what had put him in this dark mood, but she hated seeing him this way. She grabbed the broom from his hands and put it to the side. "This can wait until later. Let's go to the park now. I have a feeling you aren't the only one who needs a little distraction."

She inclined her head toward where Toby and Tyler were staring at them from the toy area. Brian nodded. "I'll pay for what they broke."

She squeezed his arm. "I'm not worried about that."

"I'm ready to see your expert slingshot moves," she told the boys as she turned to them. She noticed they stood so close together that they were touching nearly from shoulder to hip. Was that how Brian and Brady had been as kids? She imagined it had to be hard for Brian to see his brother so happy building a life on his own, and so far away. She certainly understood the feeling of being left behind.

"We're really sorry," Tyler said, swiping a hand across his cheek.

Toby nodded and looked from her to Brian. "We'll listen to you next time. Uncle Brady says we have to use our listening ears more often."

"He's a smart guy." Brian leaned in like he was telling them a secret. "He gets that from me." Both boys smiled and Emmaline noticed there was a lightness in their steps as they walked toward the front door.

She wanted that same lightness for Brian. She flipped the closed sign and turned off the lights, hoping she could be the one to give it to him.

Chapter Eleven

"Are you sure about this?" Brian asked as he pulled up to his brother's house an hour later. Emmaline glanced at him as she smoothed a stray lock of hair away from her forehead.

"Sure." She sounded not sure at all. "I appreciate Harper inviting me to dinner."

The boys had already climbed out of the car and Brian glanced into the back seat to see a sticky fruit snack smashed into the buttery leather. "Is it possible to have kids and also nice things?"

Emmaline laughed. "Typically, not if you want them to stay nice."

"I can remember one time my brother and I both

got sick in the back of my mom's station wagon after we gorged on cotton candy at the carnival."

"That's unfortunate, and this is a really lovely car," Emmaline told him. "Luckily, the boys won't have access to it for long. I'm sure you'll be able to get it detailed once you get back to Buffalo."

Hearing that phrase on her tongue pulled him up short. Back to Buffalo. Was she counting the days until he left? After his surly mood this afternoon, he wouldn't blame her. It had been easy to get aggravated by Toby and Tyler, but the truth was that Brian had been most irritated with himself. And he couldn't even share the real reason. This morning, his boss had started talking to him about plans for when he returned and how he wanted Brian to take a bigger role in the agency, which would mean giving up some of his freedom and remote-working status.

It was a great opportunity and the culmination of years of hard work but one Brian hadn't expected to materialize right now. Until the moment his boss mentioned it, Brian hadn't realized he'd unconsciously been thinking about what might happen if he stayed in Rambling Rose. One of the perks of his job was that he'd always known he could work from anywhere. Yes, he went into the office on occasion and met with clients around the country, but it had never been a big deal, because he'd never worried about anyone but himself.

As much as he appreciated the way Emmaline had tried to coax him from his bad mood and the finesse with which she handled his nephews, Brian couldn't share any of that with her. For all he knew, she wouldn't want him to stay. They had made an arrangement to be together for his temporary stay in town. She made it clear that her priority was Rosebud Antiques and her baby. He had no idea if she'd even want to make room in her life for him long term.

That thought made it feel like he was a cartoon character with a black cloud constantly hovering over him. He wasn't sure he wanted to trust Emmaline with his heart or that he was even ready to make the level of commitment a woman like her deserved. There were so many complications in both of their lives, and the way he felt so out-of-control around her terrified him. Hell, he'd practically had to sprint from her apartment to keep his desire in check. He didn't recognize this version of himself.

The time in the park had eased his worries a bit. It wasn't fair to take his mood out on anybody else. Toby and Tyler had so much infectious energy that it was hard to stay grumpy for long in their presence.

He wished he'd reacted better when the pitcher broke at the shop. He'd apologized for getting upset so many times that Emmaline had finally placed her hand over his mouth and told him she wanted to hear no more talk about broken glass. He'd obliged her.

Now he got out of the car and opened the door for her, and they followed the boys to the house.

As they approached the porch, Emmaline took his hand. "Are you really upset about Toby and Tyler messing up your car?" she asked softly.

How was this woman able to read him so easily?

"No. You're right that it can be cleaned, and at this point, I don't even care." He turned to her. "I'm going to miss those two little squirts when I'm gone. It's easier to think about all the reasons I like my uncomplicated, unsticky life back in Buffalo than to focus on the things I'm going to miss from Rambling Rose."

You most of all, he thought but didn't say out loud. Singing to her baby was one thing, but revealing how much he'd already fallen for Emmaline was quite another.

"Is she having second thoughts?"

At the sound of a male voice, Brian looked toward the front door, where his brother stood, arms crossed over his chest. A knowing grin played around the corners of Brady's mouth. "Because you did tell her she's having dinner with your more attractive brother, right? In fact, all of your brothers are more attractive than you." He looked at Emmaline as he pointed toward Brian. "That one got dumped off the ugly truck, unfortunately."

Emmaline laughed, which Brian knew was the reaction Brady was going for. His brother had an uncanny ability to put people at ease. It's what made him so great at his job as a concierge. Customer service was his superpower.

Maybe Brian should have turned the other way. Obviously Brady was happily married so there was no chance of Emmaline falling for him the way several of the girls Brian had been interested in back in high school had. But he'd grown tired of playing backup to his gregarious brother. He liked how he felt with Emmaline, and he had a sense that watching Brady work his magic wasn't going to do anything for Brian's mood.

"Thanks so much for inviting me," Emmaline said.

Brady's affable smile widened. "It's us who should be thanking you. I was sure this one would get bored of small-town life and I'd have to chain him to the house to make sure he stayed until the baby is born. Especially since babies aren't his thing. So we appreciate you helping with the boys and with the mystery of the horse sculpture. Need to keep Bri-ski busy."

Nothing about Emmaline's outward appearance changed, but Brian felt the shift in her. The last thing he needed was his brother mentioning that he wasn't into kids. Even if it was the truth.

"Just remember who kept your boys entertained so you could take your wife on a honeymoon," he told his brother, giving him a quick jab to the ribs as they walked past.

"I do appreciate it," Brady said. "And I hear congratulations are in order to you, Emmaline. Our babies will be growing up together."

Her shoulders seemed to soften slightly. "Yes. That will be nice."

They walked into the kitchen, and Harper greeted Emmaline with an enthusiastic hug. "Best friends," she exclaimed. "They aren't just going to grow up together. Our kids are going to be best friends. I know it."

"That's such a sweet thing for you to say." Emmaline's voice sounded a little wobbly. "You'll have to give me all the newborn scoop."

Harper squeezed her arms. "Definitely. We are in this together."

"See, bro?" Brady chucked Brian on the arm. "You're gonna miss all the fun."

"Leave him be," Harper scolded gently. "Not everybody thinks parenting talk is fun."

Before he could answer, Harper led Emmaline toward the kitchen table. Brian could hear her sharing the details of her earlier doctor's visit.

He glanced at his brother. "I'm not categorically opposed to parenting talk."

Brady chuckled. "No one would blame you if you are."

"Uncle Brady," Tyler called from upstairs. "Toby dropped Luke Skywalker down the heating vent. Can you help me get it?"

"On my way," Brady answered, smiling at Brian's confused expression. "His Luke Skywalker action figure."

He tugged Brian with him toward the stairs. "Let's do the switch."

A knot of anxiety immediately formed in Brian's gut. "That's a stupid idea."

"It's perfect timing. Come on," Brady urged. "It's not like I expect her to get it right. Harper is still the only person who's ever not been fooled. But it's tradition. You have to do it."

Brian knew he didn't have to do anything. He was a grown man and switching clothes with his brother to try to trick Emmaline seemed like a terrible idea. But he could hear the challenge in Brady's voice. His twin was inordinately proud that Harper hadn't even paused before calling the two of them out on their old game. Brian had been impressed by her certainty, and truthfully, he didn't want Emmaline to fail.

He had no reason to believe that she'd be able to tell them apart. Yes, he'd grown close to her in the past couple of weeks, but it wasn't as if she was in love with him or anything.

He could tell that Brady wasn't going to take no for an answer, especially after he shared the plan with Toby and Tyler, who thought it was a great idea. Although they were identical, Brady made sure that the barber cut their hair in slightly different styles so that he couldn't be fooled. It was a subtle difference, and Brian wasn't even sure the boys realized what their adoptive father was doing.

After Brady retrieved the toy from the heating duct, he and Brian exchanged clothes. They checked each other's appearance and made sure that neither of them had a hair out of place before heading back downstairs. Toby grabbed Brian's hand.

"Come on, Daddy," he said and Brian smiled in spite of himself. Or in spite of his trepidation. He supposed it was harmless fun, although the continued tightness in his stomach didn't feel like fun.

He saw Harper's eyes widen slightly, but she didn't give them away as they approached. "I hope you like fajitas," he said to Emmaline. "The grill master is back in town."

She sat on the sofa facing Harper and glanced at him as Toby climbed up next to her. "Uh, sure…" Her voice broke off, and her gaze traveled up and down Brian. "Why are you wearing your brother's clothes?"

"I don't know what you mean."

"Those are Uncle Brady's clothes," Toby told her.

"Exactly my point." She gave the boy a funny look. "Tell your Uncle Brian that I'm not so easily tricked."

Toby hesitated for a long moment then turned to Brady. "Uncle Brian, Emmaline says—"

"The real Brian," she interrupted. She placed her fingers on Toby's head and turned him in the direction of Brian.

"Oh, man." Toby let out a dejected sigh. "She's as good as Aunt Harper at telling you two apart."

Brady clapped and then bowed, first toward Emmaline and then his wife. "Well done, both of you. Is it a pregnancy thing? Does it give you a sixth sense for telling twins apart?"

"You're just different," Emmaline said with a laugh. "I can't explain it, but I know."

She knew.

Brian felt something shift in his chest as the

ball of tension loosened. He didn't spend too long questioning what that signified but quickly bent and pressed a kiss to Emmaline's mouth. She had no way of knowing how much it meant to him that she hadn't mistaken him for his brother.

By the time the evening at Brady and Harper's house was winding to a close, Emmaline felt raw with emotion. Most of it came from happiness.

She'd had such a good time with Brian and his brother's family. But her happiness had an edge to it, like a smooth road littered with shards of glass. Because being with Brady, Harper and the twins and seeing how relaxed Brian was with his family made her wish for things she knew she couldn't have.

She didn't resent Harper for her happy marriage and her sweet family. The other woman was far too kind and generous for that. But Emmaline wished for the same thing for herself.

She didn't know how or when that could ever happen, especially when it was becoming more obvious by the moment that she'd given her heart to Brian. Suddenly it felt as though a sparrow had taken flight inside her chest, its wings flitting against her rib cage as it struggled to be free. How could she have allowed herself to be so reckless when she knew she had to stay strong for her daughter.

A part of her still wanted to believe he'd come to see that he belonged in Rambling Rose. He belonged with her. But that was fanciful and foolish, and Emmaline had been sure she'd left her days of being a fool behind her.

It was clear that Brady wanted him to stay as well. He must have mentioned at least a dozen potential companies that Brian could target for marketing to gain new clients in Texas for his firm.

But whether Brian was being purposely ignorant or he really didn't see Rambling Rose as a viable option for his future, he didn't once take the bait.

Emmaline was left with Brady in the kitchen as Harper and Brian took the boys up to get ready for bed.

"Was I too obvious?" Brady asked as he took a beer from the refrigerator.

She knew exactly what he meant. "I don't think so," she said, "but I also don't think it's going to make a difference." She laughed softly. "I'm not sure why I even want it to. Brian made it clear from the start that he was leaving after your baby is born. I should respect that."

"Maybe," Brady agreed, and disappointment spiked through her. "Has he told you about his engagement?"

She didn't know quite how to answer. Obviously

Brady probably knew Brian better than anyone in the world, but the things he shared with Emmaline had been in confidence. She didn't want to break that.

Brady held up a hand. "You don't have to answer. It's good that you're not. He needs somebody loyal who puts him first. His ex-girlfriend never did. But she certainly did a number on him when she left. When you're a twin, you get used to sharing everything. People see the two of us as one unit. Brian's relationship might have been the first thing that truly belonged to him alone. That meant something to him. He doesn't trust people easily, and his natural instinct is to be reserved. When she left him, she did more than break his heart. She made him feel like he couldn't trust anyone, even himself."

"Why are you telling me this?" Emmaline asked. She traced a finger around the rim of her water glass. "Do you think I'm going to hurt him? Because I would never do that."

Brady studied her. "I can tell you really care for him, and that means something to me. It means something to all of us. I can also tell he cares for you. From what he said, the two of you have some sort of arrangement where things are going to end once he leaves."

"It makes the most sense for both of us."

"From what I've witnessed tonight," Brady said slowly, "it also means that my brother is going to be hurt again."

"He's not the only one," Emmaline murmured. She forced herself to look at Brady. "Are you warning me away from your brother?"

"Not exactly." Brady took a long pull on his beer. "I haven't seen him as happy and relaxed as he is with you in a long time. Maybe ever. I guess I'm wondering out loud why it has to end."

Emmaline had wondered the same thing countless times in recent days, but she didn't appreciate hearing it from Brady. As if she was the one in control.

"Brian and I are having fun together," she said simply. "I don't think either of us is ready for more." She wanted to confide in Brady that Brian had said he didn't even really like kids other than his two nephews, but that felt petty.

It hurt, though, and it embarrassed her to be falling for a guy who didn't want to be a father when she was only months away from having her baby. As if her daughter knew she was the topic of Emmaline's thoughts, there was a hard kick against her ribs. At her last routine appointment, her blood pressure had been slightly elevated. The doctor had cautioned her about too much stress and encouraged her to make sure she was staying hydrated and rested.

The conversation with Brady did not fall into the category of calming. Harper and Brian came down the stairs at that moment, and she forced a deep breath and tried to relax.

"Is anyone up for a game of cards?" Harper asked as she moved into the kitchen.

"I don't think so." Emmaline kept her gaze on her water glass as she placed it in the sink, willing her tumbling emotions under control before she turned back to the rest of the group. "Thank you again for dinner, but I've had a long day. I should head home." She glanced at Brian, who was studying her with an obvious frown. "Would you mind taking me?"

"Of course I'll take you." His hands fisted at his sides as he looked between her and his twin. "What did you say to her?" he demanded of Brady.

"Your brother didn't say anything," Emmaline offered before Brady could speak. "Really, Brian. This has been such a lovely evening. I'm just tired."

Harper came forward and wrapped her in a tight hug. "We'll have to do it again soon," she promised.

"Thank you again. This night meant a lot to me," she answered, which was the truth.

She and Brian didn't speak as he drove her through the darkened streets.

"Tell me what he said," Brian eventually demanded as he pulled to the curb in front of the shop. "Please."

"Nothing bad. Brady cares about you, and I think he's hoping you'll consider staying long term in Rambling Rose."

"Brady knows that isn't going to happen." A muscle ticked in Brian's jaw. "He and I are different people, Em. Maybe you got the short end of the stick with me."

"Don't say that. I like you. Just the way you are, Brian." It was the same thing he'd said to her, and she hoped it would have the same effect on him. "Do you want to come in?"

He shook his head. "Not tonight. I know you're tired and I should let you get a good night's sleep without me hogging the covers."

She'd reveal herself to be a pathetic fool if she admitted that sleeping with him was her favorite thing to do these days.

She stretched across the console and placed a gentle kiss on his cheek. "I'll talk to you tomorrow, okay?"

"Do you want go to Austin with me?" he blurted then ran a hand through his hair. "I know I asked once before, but maybe you've changed your mind.

I've been putting off a trip to that bank to try to figure out what secrets the safe deposit box holds. I'd like a break from my family, and we could make a night of it."

Maybe she should say no again. Maybe she should cut things off before it got too serious for either of them. If it was going to end, wouldn't it be easier if it ended sooner rather than later?

Every self-preservation instinct Emmaline had disappeared as she witnessed the hopefulness that transformed Brian's face from hard angles to boyish exuberance.

"I'd love to go with you," she said. "Let me see if Rebecca can help me in the store tomorrow. She covers things sometimes when my mom's busy. I think a night away sounds perfect, and even better if it's with you."

Chapter Twelve

Brian was packing his overnight bag the next morning when Brady appeared in the doorway of the guest bedroom.

"I didn't hear you come in last night," his brother said. "I thought maybe you'd spent the night at Emmaline's."

"Nope." After Brian had dropped her off, he'd driven the dark country highways around Rambling Rose until his temper cooled. By the time he got back to Brady and Harper's house, the lights were out and he was able to avoid any sort of awkward conversation with his twin. He wished he could avoid it even now.

"I can tell you really like her."

"She's a very likable person," Brian agreed, not looking up from his packing.

"I don't want to see either of you get hurt."

"Not planning on that happening," Brian lied. It was going to hurt like hell to leave Emmaline, but there was no way he'd share that with his brother right now.

"I didn't mean to overstep last night," Brady said with a long sigh. "Does it help if I say I want you to be happy?"

"Not one bit." Brian zipped up the duffel and turned to his twin. "I'm a grown man, Brady, and I've managed fine on my own since you left Buffalo. I don't need you mothering me and sure as hell not with Emmaline. My relationship with her is none of your business."

"You know…" Brady tapped on the sides of the doorframe with his palms. "When Toby and Tyler talked about her on the phone, I didn't think much of it. Then we got back and Belle was all atwitter with news that she'd introduced you to your new girlfriend."

"We're dating," Brian clarified. "I'm not sure I'd call her my girlfriend."

Brady leveled him with a stony look. "That's what I'm talking about. You've been playing this off since we got back, but I saw you with her, Bri."

"So what?"

"I know you and I know what you look like when you're in deep with a woman."

"There's no *deep* with Emmaline." Brian tried not to fidget under his brother's scrutiny. "It's temporary." In truth, he suspected he was in a serious free fall over a cliff the size of the Grand Canyon.

"You can deny it all you want. Hell, she didn't even hesitate in telling us apart. That means something."

"Stop making that some kind of benchmark. It's a stupid, immature party trick."

"It's a sign."

Brian muttered a curse. "The next thing I know you're going to be talking like Belle about true love and soul mates. This is real life."

"People fall in love in real life," his brother reminded him. "Have you thought about staying? Have you talked to her about—"

"There's nothing to talk about. Emmaline has already told me she's not looking for anything serious. She wants to concentrate on the antique shop and her baby."

"You can help with that."

"Did you slam your head into the wall on the way up here?" Brian stepped forward. "I'm not dad material, Brady. That's your gig."

"Why? You did a fine job with Toby and Tyler."

"I kept them alive for a couple of days." He let down his guard for a moment, allowed his brother to see what was behind the casual mask he normally presented to the world. "You know what happens when I fall in love. It's too much. I'm too intense."

"That was a line of bull Tammy handed you because she wanted to get out of feeling bad for the lousy way she treated you. Some women want to be loved that way."

"Emmaline is independent," Brian explained. "She's used to doing things on her own and taking care of herself. I highly doubt she'd want to deal with me on a long-term basis."

"God, your ex did a number on you."

Brian didn't deny it, although it wasn't just his Tammy who'd taught him the hard lesson of giving too much of himself. There had been so many times when he'd put forth a real effort only to fall short—with friends or girls or sports teams. Things came effortlessly for Brady, at least that's what Brian always thought. He knew his brother had struggled with the twins and making things work with Harper, but Brady seemed so capable in every area. Life came easier for Brian when he didn't try so hard. Putting himself out there was the quickest way to get shot down, and he'd had more than his share of that.

"I'm fine," he told his brother. "I appreciate your concern, but I'm not your tagalong project to handle any longer. I can manage things for myself, including Emmaline."

Brady stepped away from the door. "Well, just know that if you pull your head out of your…if you decide you're ready for a change," he said, "I'm here to support you."

"Thanks," Brian managed. He didn't like the way he felt in the face of his brother's words. He didn't like the thought that Brady was right.

On the way to Emmaline's, he called his boss and they talked about a new client who Brady was scheduled to start courting. The company was based out of Denver, and his boss wanted him to fly up for a meeting. Brady thought he could handle it over the phone, but his boss insisted.

Maybe it wouldn't be such a bad thing after all. He could get away with Emmaline and then create a little space between himself and his know-it-all brother with a quick trip to Colorado.

Emmaline was waiting just outside the antique shop. She looked lovely in a knee-length dress in a soft blue color and chunky boots, her auburn hair loose around her shoulders. It amazed him to think he hadn't realized she was pregnant that first night when they'd met or even when he'd come to the store. Impending motherhood was such an integral part of her. He'd never given much thought to the old adage of the pregnancy glow, but she definitely had it.

"I'm excited for Austin," she said as she got into the car. "We have to eat at Franklin's. If you like barbecue, that is."

"It sounds great," he said as he headed for the highway that led out of town. "I looked online and there's a band playing at a venue near the hotel. I thought if you were up for it tonight, we could catch a concert."

She grinned. "That would be amazing. There's not a lot of opportunity for live music in Rambling Rose. One thing I miss about living in Houston is all the options for entertainment." She grimaced as she glanced over at him. "Not that I took advantage of a lot of it, but I liked having choices."

"Agreed," he said. "There's always something going on in Buffalo as well. Although my family seems determined to put Rambling Rose on the map."

"Which I appreciate."

Brian glanced into the back of the car. He'd placed the horse sculpture on the seat, wrapped in a towel.

Emmaline followed his gaze. "You seat belted it in," she said with smile.

"I was going to put it in the trunk, but it felt

like the thing was looking at me, begging to be in the mix."

"You really are a softy. You let Toby and Tyler make a mess of your leather, and now the horse is along for the ride."

"Isn't that what uncles are for? Especially out-of-town uncles. I've got to make my mark while I have the time."

Her smile faded, and he could have kicked himself for mentioning the fact that he was leaving. Obviously they both knew it, but the point of this trip was having fun in the present moment.

She reached across the console and squeezed his hand. "I'm glad we're doing this."

Brian blew out a breath he hadn't realized he was holding, affection for Emmaline blooming in his chest at her ability to keep things positive. He turned on the radio to an oldies station and they sang along as they drove.

It was a gorgeous day with blue skies above them and the sun shining high in the winter sky. Once again, Brian was amazed by the wide-open landscape of Texas. It felt bigger. They passed several trucks driven by men in Stetson hats. One of the oversize rigs even had a bumper sticker with the outline of the state of Texas with a Colorado flag in the center. It made him think about the potential client in Denver.

He talked to Emmaline about some of his ideas, and she gave great feedback. He liked the new creativity he'd discovered since arriving in Texas, as if the change of scenery recharged him.

By the time they got to the bank parking lot, most of his frustrations over the conversation with Brady had disappeared. They walked into the building, which was decorated in a traditional Southwestern style, with soft beige walls, wood accents and various cowboy-themed paintings.

Brian asked to see the banker that Emmaline's customer had suggested, and they were shown to an office at the end of a long hall.

A balding man with a bushy beard stood from behind an antique cherry desk. "I'm Henry Gilday," the man said. "How can I help you?"

Brian introduced himself, then explained the reason for his visit. "We were told that this key comes from a safe deposit box at your bank." He pulled the tarnished key from his pocket and held it up.

"Ah, yes." Henry Gilday nodded. "Austin Savings Bank has been serving this community for almost a hundred years now."

"Are you saying the key is that old?" Emmaline asked. Brian could hear the excitement in her voice, and it added to his own. There was no telling what secrets the safe deposit box might hold.

"Not necessarily." Henry held out a hand, and Brian dropped the key into it.

"But you do think the key opens a safe deposit box here in the bank?"

"Yes."

"Can we try it?"

Henry glanced up from the key. "No."

Brian didn't like hearing the word no. "I don't understand. I have the key that opens a box in your vault. There's a bit of a mystery involved with how this key came into our possession and—"

"That's exactly why not," Henry explained. "I have no legal record of the box being registered to your name."

"Right," Brian agreed. "Because we found the key in the base of a sculpture my brother was given as a gift. I'd like to track down the person who sent that sculpture."

"I'm afraid I can't help you with that or take you to the vault." Henry handed the key back to Brian, and he closed his fist around the metal.

"Can you tell me who the box is registered to at least?" Brian's mind raced as he tried to come up with solutions to this latest roadblock on his quest to discover who'd sent Brady and Harper the horse.

"No." Henry sighed. "Our privacy protocols are strict."

Disappointment pounded through Brian. "I

called last week and the woman who I talked to, Jessica, said that I could probably get into the box."

"She shouldn't have told you that. Some of these young hires are more concerned with making sure they get five stars on the automated survey at the end of the call than actually telling customers something they might not want to hear." He tapped one thick finger on the edge of the desk. "You said you got the key in some sort of sculpture?"

"It's an Alonzo Flynn piece," Emmaline added.

"I've heard of him." Henry nodded. "If you can get written approval from whoever owns the box to let you in, then that's a different story."

"We don't know who owns the box." Brian tried to keep the frustration out of his voice, but he could feel it seeping into every one of his cells. He'd hoped to finish up the business at the bank, then check into the hotel with Emmaline and take her out to dinner and some live music to celebrate solving the mystery. Now he just felt even more inept because he believed what the other woman had told him.

"Your best bet might be to track down the dealer who sold the sculpture," the banker suggested.

Brian understood the man was trying to be helpful, but he'd spent hours trying to locate the origin of the sculpture to no avail. His pulse calmed slightly when Emmaline took his hand in hers.

"Thank you," she said to Henry Gilday. "Do

you have a direct line so we can contact you if we have any luck with finding whoever owns the safe deposit box?"

"Of course," the man answered. He went behind his large desk and pulled out a business card. "I'll give you my cell phone number as well."

"This is a beautiful piece," Emmaline said as she ran a finger along the top of the dark wood desk. "Is it eighteenth century?"

"As a matter of fact, it is." Henry beamed as he handed over the card. "It belonged to my great-grandfather. Do you have an interest in antiques?"

"I do. I run a shop in Rambling Rose that once belonged to my grandfather. It's small but—"

"You should check out her website," Brian suggested. "Rosebudantiques.com. She has an amazing eye."

"I just might. Please let me know if you find out anything else or if I can be of additional help. Sorry I couldn't give you what you wanted today."

Brian blew out a deep breath. Yes, it was frustrating not to get what he came for, but he still had an entire afternoon and evening to spend with Emmaline. That would make the trip worth it no matter what.

Emmaline tapped her foot along to the country band later that night. After checking into the hotel, she and Brian had done some sightseeing around Austin and then gone to dinner at her favorite barbecue joint. She stifled a yawn as Brian returned to the table with her glass of root beer. She didn't want him to think she wasn't enjoying herself, but she really could have used a nap that afternoon. He'd offered, but she was too afraid to take him up on it.

They were sharing a hotel room and her physical awareness of him and the need that pulsed through her every time he looked at her had only grown in the past week. When she'd agreed to the trip to Austin, she hadn't thought about what would happen at the end of the night.

Although his kisses drove her wild, Brian had been true to his word of not staying the night at her apartment and things hadn't progressed in the way Emmaline secretly wanted. Not that she blamed him. She appreciated that he was trying to be a gentleman, but part of her wondered if he just didn't like the thought of being with somebody in her condition.

She kept going today because she didn't want to embarrass herself by pushing for more than he was ready to give, but now she was tired.

"What do you think about heading back after the next song?" he asked as he slid into the chair next to her.

Would she ever get used to how well he could read her? Or would it even matter since he'd be leaving after his new niece or nephew was born?

"That would probably be for the best," she said. "I'm sorry to be such a dud date."

He linked their fingers. "I have more fun with you than I've ever had with anyone." The sweetness of his tone made butterflies flit across her middle. The band switched from a lively party song to a slow ballad. Brian stood and tugged her up with him. "One dance and then we'll head out?"

She nodded and followed him to the dance floor. It was hard to believe that it was nearly a month ago when she'd first met him. As exciting as that night had been for her, now it felt exactly right for him to put his arms around her and draw her close. She rested her head on his shoulder and closed her eyes as the singer crooned about the one who got away.

Oh, how Emmaline could already relate to that.

When the song was over, they left the bar arm in arm. "Are you okay walking?" Brian asked. Their hotel was only a few blocks away.

It was a crisp, clear night, and Emmaline figured she could use a little bit of cooling down before returning to their room.

They were crossing the street when a familiar voice called her name. She turned to see Robert, her ex-boyfriend, crossing in the other direction with a group of guys she didn't recognize.

Her heart seemed to stop in her chest as his eyes grew wide and his gaze lowered to her stomach. She'd changed into a long black dress, which hugged her belly as well as a denim jacket to ward off the evening chill and a bright turquoise necklace around her neck.

Robert met them on the corner and she could feel Brian's questioning gaze on her. But she could barely draw a breath, let alone figure out how to introduce him to her ex.

"This is a surprise," she said, which might have been the understatement of the year.

"Yeah," Robert agreed. "I took a new job, and I'm doing training in Austin. You look…"

"Beautiful," Brian supplied when it was clear Robert couldn't manage to complete the sentence. "She's beautiful."

"Right," her ex agreed, running a hand through his hair and glancing between her and Brian. Was his hair thinning? Emmaline studied him more closely. Had he always had that little paunch in front?

Had she just settled without a second thought? She wasn't exactly the type of person to get fixated on someone's outward appearance, although Robert hadn't been a great boyfriend across the board. Staying with him had been just one more way she'd made herself small.

It's what she'd learned from years of watching her mom struggle to find happiness with a man.

She wasn't quite sure she was making a better choice now. Brian might treat her well and make her feel special, but he would be leaving soon, and then she'd be alone.

And heartbroken.

One of the other guys from Robert's group called to him.

"I should go," he said, still appearing stunned. "I could give you a call, Emmie. We might—"

"I don't think so," she interrupted. She might not be making the best choice for her future, but she wasn't going to settle. Not when her daughter would be watching her the way she had her mom. "But I'm glad to see you, Robert."

"Yeah?" he asked, sounding surprised and hopeful.

"It reminds me that I need to schedule a meeting with my attorney. I'll be sending you the forms to sign to relinquish your parental rights early next week."

"Forms," he repeated dully.

"You'll sign them," she said, making her tone certain. "There will be no question that you have no rights to my baby."

His mouth dropped open, but he didn't argue. "Um, I have to go."

"Robert." She grabbed his arm as he turned away. "Tell me you are going to sign the papers."

He stared at her for a lengthy moment, and she wondered why she'd stayed with him for as long as she had. She felt nothing for him but apathy.

"Pregnancy has changed you," he said.

"For the better," she agreed, keeping her tone cool.

"I'll sign whatever you send over," he agreed. "Good luck, Emmie."

"Goodbye, Robert," she murmured and watched him walk away.

Chapter Thirteen

Emmaline listened to the clip of her boots against the sidewalk as she and Brian walked in silence the rest of the way to the hotel. She appreciated that he didn't fill the weighted quiet with words, because she wasn't sure she could manage to speak without breaking down.

She didn't want to get emotional about her ex-boyfriend. He didn't deserve that kind of power over her. In some ways, seeing Robert tonight had been a blessing. She knew she needed to move forward on the legal documents that would ensure he relinquished his parental rights to her baby.

When she'd told her mother her plan, Krista had

nodded in agreement. Emmaline knew from growing up with a single mom that she never wanted to worry whether her baby's father would try to return and exert some influence in her child's life. Her dad had never truly been a part of her life other than cards and gifts that didn't mean anything each year on her birthday.

Emmaline knew that if at some point her daughter chose to have a relationship with her father and Robert wanted that, Emmaline wouldn't stop it. But she wasn't going to share custody with a man who had made it clear the life growing inside of her was nothing but a nuisance to him.

As they approached the entrance of the hotel, Brian took her hand. "If you want to pretend that didn't happen, I respect it. But know that I'm here if you need to talk or vent or whatever." He took a strand of her hair between two fingers, studying it like he was fascinated. "I'm here for you, Emmaline. You and the baby."

She looked up into his dark eyes, and her heart flipped in her chest. He'd become so important to her despite all of her big, internal lectures to herself about keeping things casual. There was nothing casual about how she felt for Brian.

"That was necessary," she murmured. "Not exactly the timing I would have chosen, but it feels like some closure. I can have the documents sent to him next week."

"And you believe he'll sign?"

"Yes. I have no doubt he wants nothing to do with me or this baby."

Brian looked away for a long moment, and when he glanced back at her, she could see the fire in his eyes. "Then, he's a fool."

"Maybe," Emmaline agreed. "I'd rather have him be honest than to pretend he wanted a life with me when he truly doesn't."

A muscle ticked in Brian's jaw and she wondered for a brief second what he was thinking. Normally she could read him easily, but her emotions were jumbled. It was strange to be talking about her ex with the current man in her life. She wanted to call Brian her boyfriend. There was something deep inside her that longed to name this connection between them, as if that would make it real.

In all the ways that mattered, it felt real. Except that he was leaving.

"You deserve to be happy," he said. "You deserve a man who appreciates your worth and who makes you feel special. You deserve to be cherished, Em."

She swallowed around the ball of emotion lodged in her throat. She wanted him to be that man. Those were the ways he made her feel.

She didn't want to think about the end or Brian leaving. She knew it was coming. There was no denying it. But right now, she just wanted to be with him. In every way that mattered.

She leaned in and kissed him. She let all of the swirling emotions inside her release as their connection deepened. She wanted him to know how she felt without having to say it out loud.

He responded exactly as she wanted him to. He slanted his mouth over hers and pulled her closer until she was enveloped in the heat of him.

They stayed wrapped in each other's arms for several minutes. When she finally pulled back, need and desire were reflected in his gaze.

"You're amazing," he whispered. She felt amazing at this moment. Her past didn't matter and the future would be there to deal with later.

"The same could be said about you," she told him, then darted a glance at a group of people passing. "So much so that I've apparently forgone my personal rule against public displays of affection."

He brushed another quick kiss against her lips. "Is that an actual rule of yours?"

"Before you, it was."

"I'm turning you into a rebel." He laughed softly and his gaze smoldered. "I like the sound of that."

"Let's go upstairs." Nerves flickered through her, and she hoped he'd gather her meaning.

"Yes," he agreed and linked their fingers. "But so you know—"

"I want to be with you, Brian," she interrupted, afraid if she wasn't clear that she'd lose her nerve once they got to the room. As much as she appreciated his tendency to act like a gentleman, she wanted more tonight. Everything he could give her.

She thought he might argue, and every cell in her body was poised to protest. But after a moment, he finally spoke.

"I want that, too," he answered and led her into the hotel.

Emmaline knew that her feet carried her across the lobby. She was fairly certain Brian had ushered her into the elevator, and they got to their room on the fourth floor.

But when she was suddenly standing a few feet from the bed—the one she'd truly share with Brian tonight—it felt like she'd been beamed up there in an instant. Blood rushed through her brain and body, causing most of her coherent thoughts to disappear like smoke in the wind before they could even fully form.

Brian locked the door and drew the curtains over the large window and then turned to her.

To Emmaline's surprise, he looked as nervous as she felt. At least she wasn't alone.

"At any point, you can change your mind."

She felt one corner of her mouth kick up. "Same goes for you."

A pained expression crossed his face. "Maybe I shouldn't admit this, but I've been thinking about little else than you and me together for weeks now. There is no chance of me having second thoughts."

Once again, she was amazed that any man—let alone one as handsome and successful as Brian—could feel that way about her. Tonight he wore a crisp button-down and dark trousers. He sported a pair of boots that weren't quite cowboy but rugged enough to make him look like he belonged in Texas. She knew without question that he belonged with her.

"I won't have second thoughts either," she promised. "You aren't the only one with an active imagination."

He looked stunned for a moment, and then his mouth spread into a wolfish grin. "Now, sweetheart, that's about the most tempting thing I've ever heard. I want you to tell me all the details that you've come up with in that brilliant mind of yours. I want to support your creativity."

Emmaline's throat went dry. Thinking illicit

thoughts in her head and sharing them out loud were two different things.

"Let's begin with the fact that you're wearing too many clothes," she told him. If she was going to live in the moment, she might as well make it one to remember.

"That's a good place to start," he agreed. He began to unbutton his shirt, and she noticed his fingers fumbling.

"Are you nervous?" She stepped toward him and unfastened the pearl buttons herself, kicking off the ballerina flats she wore at the same time.

"I've thought about this moment so many times. I want to be worthy of you, Em. I want this to be perfect."

"How can it be anything else between the two of us?"

She tugged the shirt from the waistband of his pants and he shrugged out of it. Then she ran her hands over the hard muscles of his chest, loving the feel of his skin and the way his breath hitched. He swallowed audibly and she lifted her mouth to the underside of his jaw. It was rough with end-of-day stubble. She could smell the soap he used mixed with his natural scent, and it made her crazy with need. He massaged her shoulders and then drew his nails down her back before claiming her mouth again.

She felt the cool air of the hotel room on her bare legs as he lifted her dress over her hips. She raised her arms and a moment later was standing in front of him in her bra and panties. She sucked in a breath as he reached out and teased the tips of her breasts with his thumbs.

The sensation was so overwhelming she felt her knees give way and might have slumped directly to the floor if Brian hadn't been there to catch her. He lifted her onto the bed, and the desire she could see in his eyes made heat and an answering yearning pool low in her belly. He toed off his boots as he unbuckled his belt, then pushed his pants and boxers down to the carpeted floor.

Emmaline had felt the evidence of his arousal before, but this was different. She knew how good it would be. There was no question. When he joined her on the bed, their mouths fused as he ran his hands along the length of her body. It was too much and not enough.

She groaned with pleasure as he pulled down the straps of her bra and took one taut nipple and then the other into his mouth. It was as if he knew exactly what she wanted, what she needed. Pleasure spiraled through her as he kissed a path down her body.

At this point, Emmaline was going to lose control before they even got to the main event. But

Brian seemed in no hurry, as if he really had spent weeks thinking about feasting on her body.

Her hands splayed across his shoulders, and she urged him up again. "Now," she murmured, looking deep into his eyes. "I want you now, Brian."

His nostrils flared. "I have so many plans for you."

"We've got all night," she reminded him and lifted her hips to wiggle out of her panties. "Please."

He gave a guttural moan and positioned himself between her legs. But before he entered her, he placed the sweetest kiss on each of her cheeks.

"You are beautiful," he said again.

Emmaline had never really considered herself a beauty. She was pretty enough but not exactly attractive by conventional standards.

Now she saw herself through Brian's eyes, and it was a heady feeling. So overwhelming that she felt a single tear leak from the corner of one eye.

She lifted her head and kissed him at the same time she wrapped her hands around his hips and urged him forward. He entered her in one long thrust. As good as she thought it was going to be, it was that much better.

They moved together like their bodies were made for each other. But it wasn't just that. Brian continued to cradle her face in his hands, kissing her lips and her throat. It was like he wanted to touch every inch of her, and she felt truly like he was claiming her. Or maybe she was claiming him.

Either way, pleasure built quickly inside her. When the pressure slammed through her, shattering her nerves into a million pieces, she cried out his name. He held her as the shudders subsided, then increased the pace of their movement. Emmaline would have thought her body had no more to give, but it responded to him like they were two sides to a magnet pulled toward each other. He gave one long cry of pleasure minutes later and then stilled without putting his weight fully on her.

She went with him as he turned and gathered her close. "I didn't expect…" How could she explain exactly how amazing that had been for her without making a total fool of herself?

"Me neither," he said and lifted her hand to his mouth. He kissed each of her knuckles in turn. "All I can say is thank the Lord we have a late checkout tomorrow. I have a feeling you're going to need to get caught up on sleep."

Delight spiraled through her. "Is that so? I guess we're going to find out how creative we can truly get."

Brian couldn't seem to wipe the smile from his face over the next several days. He'd guessed that making love to Emmaline would be amazing, but there was no way of truly understanding how close it would make him feel to her.

They'd stayed up most of the night in the Austin hotel, alternately talking and learning the details of each other's bodies. He'd gone for a run in the morning while she slept in and then ordered one of nearly everything on the breakfast menu.

He loved everything about being with her, although the fact that he was even willing to use that word secretly terrified him. Brian had only allowed himself to love one woman, and she'd broken his heart. Even though he could rationalize the fact that he and Emmaline weren't a long-term deal, it didn't stop him from wanting her that way.

A recipe for disaster, he reminded himself as he entered the Hotel Fortune lobby and waited for his brother to finish advising a couple of hotel guests. When the man and woman walked away from the concierge desk, he beckoned his twin toward him.

"Did you get a haircut?" Brady asked.

Brian shrugged. "Yeah. I was sick of people around town confusing me for you, even though I'm obviously the better-looking twin. I didn't want there to be any question."

Brady seemed to consider that. "Or is it more about the fact you didn't want Emmaline and

Harper to be the only ones who can tell us apart? Hits a little too close to home, right?"

There were times when it annoyed the hell out of Brian how well his brother knew him.

"As much fun as it is to have you overanalyze every decision I make," he said with an exaggerated eye roll, "I'm here because we found some information on the horse sculpture that might be helpful."

He pulled out his phone and unlocked the home screen to show Brady a picture of a property outside Denver that had been featured in a Colorado architectural magazine. "These people have several Alonzo Flynn sculptures, and the article mentions that the collector is a bit of a historian on the artist. I fly out first thing tomorrow morning for a night in Denver to meet with my agency's potential clients, so I called the guy and asked if he'd be willing to meet me. I'm going to bring the sculpture with me in my carry-on because I feel like if he sees the piece in person, he might take helping track down the history of it more seriously."

"You really are dedicated to this," Brady commented.

"I hate a mystery I can't solve."

"Or maybe you want a distraction from admitting that you are head over heels for the antique-shop owner." Brady held up his hands when Brian scowled. "Not that I'm complaining. I appreciate all of the help."

"This has nothing to do with Emmaline or her shop."

"Who found the collector in Colorado?" Brady lifted a brow.

"Shut up," Brian muttered.

"It's okay to admit that you like her."

"Once again, it's not a shock. Everyone who knows her likes her."

"Valentine's Day is just around the corner," Brady reminded him. "It would be quite a gift if you told her you were moving here."

Brian's stomach lurched. "I'm not sure she'd agree," he admitted. "Emmaline seems content with our arrangement just the way it is."

"Has she told you that?"

"Not exactly, but I think I know her well enough to understand what she's thinking."

Brady laughed. "It's a horrible mistake to think you ever know what goes through a woman's brain. They are way better at thinking than you or me, and we can't possibly understand the way their minds work."

Brian didn't believe that was true. Maybe it had been that way for Brady because things came easy to him. Relationships had come easy to him. Brian was an observer, and everything he'd observed in

Emmaline told him that she was strong enough not to need anyone, especially him. So if he allowed himself to be truly vulnerable with her, he also knew where that would lead.

"I'm going to stay at her apartment tonight," he told his brother. "And head to the airport from there in the morning. I'll check in with you after I speak with the collector."

"Thanks, man. And about what I said… I'm not going to hazard a guess at what Emmaline is thinking, but I can say for sure Harper, the boys and I like having you here."

Brian nodded. That meant something, but was he ready to take the chance of staking a claim in Rambling Rose if he truly had no future with Emmaline? He was only just beginning to imagine a life in Texas, but he knew he wouldn't want one without her.

After leaving Hotel Fortune, he waved to a few people as he walked toward the antique shop, as usual amazed at what a tight-knit community this small town was and how easily he felt like he'd become part of the fabric of it. Maybe it was because there were so many Fortunes in town already, but Brian had never had this sense of place in Buffalo, even though he'd spent his entire life there.

Emmaline was just flipping the sign on the door to closed as he approached. The smile she gave him did funny things to his insides. He thought about what his brother had told him. Maybe he was being foolish to assume he knew what she was thinking. She certainly looked at him like she wanted more than just the next couple of weeks.

They walked upstairs and put together a simple dinner of pasta with a homemade carbonara sauce. He'd miss these quiet nights with her as well. She told him about her day and the call she'd received about a barn full of old furniture that had been recently discovered in a small town about an hour east of Rambling Rose.

Her excitement was contagious, and it made him want to cancel his Denver trip so he could drive with her tomorrow to check it out. Then he reminded himself she didn't need his help to do her job. She rarely needed his help with anything. But as they finished cleaning up from dinner, his eye caught on a small toolbox she'd stashed next to the counter.

"Home repairs?" he asked, gesturing toward it.

"I'm determined to get the crib put together this week. It will feel like I'm somewhat ready."

"Let's do it tonight," he suggested. "And we can paint the room this weekend after I'm back from Denver."

She scrunched up her nose. "You can't really

want to spend your evening assembling nursery furniture."

"Sure I do. If it helps you, then it's a good use of my time." He took her hand and tugged her closer, wrapping his arms around her shoulders. He loved the way she fit against him. All of her curves and the sweet swell of her belly. "I care about you, Em. A lot."

He felt a tremble race through her and wondered at her reaction to his words. He might not be able to fully decipher her mind, but her body communicated plenty.

"Me too," she whispered, and they stood together for several silent moments.

Just as he'd noticed that tremble, Brian felt immediately when something inside her changed. He imagined her mind had taken control of her body and heart. He certainly could relate to that struggle.

She pulled away, and the smile she gave him didn't quite reach her eyes. "Then, let's get to work," she said with forced cheer.

He wanted to share the conversation he'd had with Brady. This was the moment to put it all on the line, but fear held him back. He grabbed the toolbox from the wood floor and followed her to the nursery. She turned on the radio, and they worked on the crib.

Brian took care with every step because the crib was important. It's where Emmaline's baby would sleep, so he needed it to be perfect. Even if he wasn't ever going to be around to see the girl lay her head there. After they finished, Emmaline unwrapped the mattress that was propped against one wall. She placed it in the crib and covered it with a pink sheet in a chevron pattern.

"It's perfect," she said softly and he nodded, pleased despite the ache in his chest that he had some involvement in helping her get ready for the baby's arrival.

He wondered if months from now she'd think about him when she lay her daughter down to sleep.

"This weekend we'll paint," he said definitively. "And then you'll be ready."

She laughed. "I'm not sure I'll ever be fully ready. Although I already have so many plans for her."

"She's a lucky girl." Brian ran a hand through his hair. This was the moment that he should tell her he wanted more. He wasn't sure how to define what he felt for Emmaline or whether he could truly give her what she needed, but he never would if he didn't put himself out there to try. He simply wasn't ready to risk it.

He could feel her studying him as if she sensed

the battle warring inside of him. He opened his mouth to speak but yawned instead. Brady would get a big laugh out of his anxiety, but Brian just couldn't bring himself to share the things that were in his heart. Not when he was so unsure what her reaction would be.

"I should probably get to bed if that's okay with you," he told her. "I've got to take off for the airport early tomorrow."

"Sure. I understand." Emmaline picked up the hammer and screwdriver they'd left on the floor, tucked them into the toolbox and carried it out of the room.

With one last glance at the crib, Brian followed, wondering why it felt like he'd just missed swinging at his best chance for a home run in the game of life.

Chapter Fourteen

"Why the hurry?" Emmaline's mother asked the following Saturday morning. From where she was perched on the ladder in the nursery, Krista turned to study her daughter.

"It's not exactly a hurry," Emmaline grumbled. "I'm seven months along now, so it's past time I finished the nursery."

"Babies aren't picky." Krista's gaze went wistful. "All I had when I brought you home from the hospital was a wicker bassinet in the corner of my bedroom. You didn't seem to mind."

"I know. But I'll feel more settled once this room is done."

"You did a good job on the crib. I'll admit I was a bit skeptical when you bought one that needed to be assembled. I guess you inherited your grandfather's handiness as well as his love for old things."

Emmaline ran a hand over the crib's wood railing. "Brian helped me before he left for Colorado." He'd been due back yesterday but had gotten delayed by a snowstorm in the Rockies.

"He helped you put the crib together but drew the line at painting?" Her mother rolled her eyes. "It figures."

"He offered to help paint when he got back." Emmaline squeezed her eyes shut for a moment. "It just didn't feel right to expect so much of him."

"Why?" Her mother stepped down from the ladder and placed the paint roller in the tray on the floor.

"Because the nursery isn't his responsibility."

"Do you want it to be?"

Emmaline turned and bent to smooth out the drop cloth she'd placed over the carpet. "It doesn't matter what I want. He's leaving once Harper has the baby."

"You fell for him."

"I did not."

"Do you love him?"

"Mom."

"Emmaline."

"He's nice. He's nice to me and he's sweet about the baby."

"What happened to casual?"

"We're casual," Emmaline muttered.

"Not if you're in love with him. That's not casual."

"I know." Emmaline threw up her hands as she swallowed back a sob. "I know what I feel for him isn't casual. I know it's stupid and probably self-destructive. I feel more for Brian after a month of being together than I have for any other man I've known."

"And he's leaving."

"Yes. I don't need you to say 'I told you so' because I've already lectured myself. That's why I asked for your help. To prove that I didn't need him. I can take care of myself and my baby all on my own."

"You don't need him," Krista agreed quietly. "But you want him."

Emmaline dashed a hand over her cheek. "How could I let this happen? I know better. You taught me better."

"Some lessons have to be learned on your own." Her mother put an arm around Emmaline's shoulder. "It's going to hurt real bad, baby girl. Trust me on that. I wish you'd listened to me, but you'll get through it. You're tough like me."

"I don't think I appreciated everything you gave up for me. I'm sorry I was—"

"You never have to apologize. The best thing that happened in my life was you. You were worth every struggle. I know my granddaughter is going to be the same."

Emmaline's heart felt close to bursting. "Thanks, Mom."

"You have to be smarter, girl. Smarter than I was. Men are a dime a dozen. Even the ones with the last name Fortune."

Emmaline didn't bother to argue with her mother. She realized how precious this support was in her life. But she also knew Brian was something special. He made her feel special. In a way that no one had before and she guessed no one would after him.

That didn't change what she needed to do. Her baby had to be her priority, and the longer she kept this going, the worse it would be. She'd known from the start that she wasn't meant for casual relationships. She just hadn't expected to fall in love so quickly. Now that she had, the only thing she could do was work on getting over it. As much as it would hurt.

She and her mother finished the painting, and then Emmaline fixed sandwiches in her small kitchen for lunch. She missed her grandfather at times like this. Sure, she missed him in the store, as well, but it was these quiet little moments that she had always enjoyed the most with him.

A knock sounded on the door just as her mother was getting ready to walk out. Emmaline opened it to find Brian standing on the other side.

He looked tired, rumpled from traveling and absolutely irresistible. Which just proved that she needed to find a way to resist him. He greeted her mom looking almost nervous. Emmaline didn't blame him. Krista had that disapproving-mother stare down pat, but then she offered Brian a small smile.

"The crib looks good," she said, which was high praise coming from Krista.

Brian seemed to realize it. He nodded and swallowed. "Thank you. I'm ready to be put to work as a painter next."

Krista arched a brow in Emmaline's direction. "You know what you have to do," she said, then headed down the stairs.

When she was gone, Brian pulled Emmaline to him. "I've missed you," he said. "You wouldn't believe how excited I am to start painting. And I have so much to tell you. The client meeting was amazing, and the mountains looked so beautiful covered in snow against the backdrop of the blue sky. Have you been to Colorado? We should go together."

Emmaline tried not to melt into him, but it was a losing battle. Her mind might be certain about what she needed to do, but her heart and her body still hadn't gotten on board with the plan. "How was your meeting with the art collector?" She pulled away and stepped farther into her apartment.

Brian shrugged. "He had some really interesting Alonzo Flynn pieces in his collection, but unfortunately not much information about our Trojan horse."

Emmaline snickered. She'd forgotten they'd nicknamed the sculpture the Trojan horse. How fitting, since it was that innocent piece of art that had brought Brian more fully into her life. She'd had no idea at the time what that would mean to her heart.

Brain studied her more closely. "What was your mom doing here? And why does it look like you have flecks of paint on your shirt?"

Emmaline smoothed a hand over her front and then cradled her stomach. It was the reminder she needed. It didn't matter if she hurt as long as she did what was best for her baby.

"My mom helped me paint the nursery," she said.

"I thought that was my job." She hated the disappointment and hesitation that had crept into Brian's voice.

Rip off the Band-Aid, she reminded herself. That was the only way to handle it.

"I think it would be better if we didn't see each other anymore." She was proud that she'd been able to say the words without her voice giving out.

Brian massaged a hand along the back of his neck and closed his eyes for several seconds. "I don't understand. Did I do something wrong? Does your mother have a problem with me?" His lips thinned. "I know I'm not the easygoing charmer that Brady is, but I can win her over. I know I can. Just give me a chance to—"

"It's not my mom." Emmaline crossed her arms over her chest. "I need to focus on the future. We both know that this thing between us is going to end."

"Is this about me going to Denver?"

"No, it's not about Denver. It's about what I need in my life."

"And what you don't need is me?"

I do need you. So much. Emmaline's heart pounded with all the things she wanted to say to him. But those things would just make her look like a bigger fool. She'd already let her heart stay in the lead for far too long.

"I'm a soon-to-be single mother living in a

small town in Texas." She pointed a finger at him. "You're a big-city bachelor who likes your freedom and your uncomplicated life. I'm a box of complications, Brian."

"The past month has seemed simple enough to me," he murmured. "Why does that have to change?"

Because I'm in love with you, she wanted to scream. But she didn't. It was bad enough that she felt as though she was dying on the inside. She couldn't bring herself to invite outright rejection from him. If he wanted more, he'd tell her.

"We've had fun," she said, which was only a tiny bit of the truth between them. "I'll keep up the research on the sculpture and let you know if I find anything."

"That's it?" He blew out a long breath.

"Is there something more?" she asked, hoping beyond hope that he'd give her some sign that her fears weren't founded. All she needed was one tiny reason to launch herself into his arms and ask him to stay.

Their gazes held, and she could almost feel the current of electricity running between them. Emmaline wanted to believe that Brian would tell her something more. That he would give her what she needed to hear, the admission of love she was too afraid to say to him.

"You're right."

Her heart seemed to shatter into a million pieces at those two words. He looked as miserable as she felt, which should have been consolation but wasn't. It didn't make her feel any better for him to be unhappy as well.

"I won't bother you anymore," he told her.

"You're not a bother."

"You know what I mean."

She did, unfortunately. There was no doubt that a clean break between them was best. Smartest, anyway.

"We'll still be friends," she suggested, even though the word sounded hollow. "Rambling Rose is a small town and I would like to be friends with Harper." A horrible thought wedged itself into her mind. "Unless you don't want that. If it's too weird for you, then I can—"

"Of course you can be friends with Harper." He tried for a smile, but it didn't come anywhere near to reaching his eyes. "She wouldn't have it any other way." He lifted a hand like he was going to reach for her then pressed it to his side again. "I want you to be happy, Emmaline. I want that more than you could know."

How was she supposed to respond? He made her happy and the thought of not having him in her life did the opposite. Her little girl kicked like she could sense her mother's stricken emotions. That kept Emmaline from hurling herself at Brian and begging him to give them a chance the way she wanted to.

"I should go get cleaned up." She picked at a fleck of dried paint stuck to her arm. "I guess I'll see you around."

"Yeah," he agreed, his voice devoid of emotion. If he said it had been nice knowing her, she felt like she might lose it, but he only nodded and walked away, the door to her apartment clicking shut behind him. She was afraid the door to her heart would be padlocked forever.

Brian walked into Kirby's Perks two days later. He knew he wouldn't see Emmaline there. Brady had told him that she and Harper had gone shopping for baby supplies that morning. He'd passed Rosebud Antiques and saw her mother talking to a customer. He thought about going in and asking Krista what she thought about her daughter's decision to remove him from her life.

But he wasn't sure he truly wanted to know. Emmaline had said her mother had nothing to do with it, but Brian suspected something different.

How was he supposed to make a case for continuing their relationship when everything she said had been right? He was leaving. It still shocked him that she was willing and able to end things so abruptly. He would have liked to believe he meant more to her than that. He should have trusted his gut. He knew what happened when he let himself care.

He waved to Martin and then Rebecca, the coffeehouse regulars, as he made his way to the counter. Kirby greeted him with a sympathetic smile.

"You look about as bad as she does," the shop owner told him.

"I'm fine," he lied. "And I'm sure she's better than fine. Or at least, she will be."

"We've missed seeing you here."

"I didn't want to intrude on a place that feels like it belongs to her." He glanced to the right and, for the first time, noticed the streamers and pink balloons that decorated one side of the cafe space. Alarmed, he looked back at Kirby, who shrugged.

"We're planning a surprise baby shower for her. Harper was in charge of the distraction because I didn't want to take the chance of Emmaline stopping in for coffee before we were ready. She needed something to cheer her up."

"She's lucky to have such great friends."

"We love her." Kirby handed him his usual black coffee and a brown bag.

"What's this?"

"Coffee and muffin on the house," she said. "It looks like you could use a bit of cheering as well."

"I should go before the party gets started. I'm the last person Emmaline would want to see here."

"You're welcome anytime, Brian."

"Thanks," he murmured, forcing the smile to remain on his face. He could do this. "There's a good chance I'll be leaving Rambling Rose sooner than expected. Probably by the end of this week." He actually had no plans to leave, but as he said the words, he knew they were right. It was too damn difficult to stay and take the chance of running into Emmaline around town.

"Oh." Kirby nodded. "Harper didn't mention that. She said you were here until her baby arrives."

"That was the plan." Brian shrugged. "But my boss needs me back in Buffalo for a couple of client meetings." He didn't mention his possible promotion because right now he wasn't in a mood to celebrate anything. "I'll fly out again when my new niece or nephew makes an appearance."

"Well, we'll look forward to seeing you then."

He nodded, then took his muffin and coffee and headed for the door. The bright sunshine of the winter morning seemed to mock him as he walked toward the hotel. He was going to have to tell Brady about his change of plans, and his twin wouldn't be happy.

Just as he got to the corner, Emmaline and Harper appeared. They didn't see him at first, so

Brian had a moment to drink in the sight of Emmaline. Her hair was pulled back in a loose bun with copper strands framing either side of her face. She smiled at something Harper said, but Brian would have sworn there were shadows under her eyes.

The same shadows that darkened his face. But he didn't take comfort in that fact. Anything that made her unhappy made him unhappy, which was why when she looked up and met his gaze, her blue eyes widening, he blurted, "I'm leaving."

Her mouth formed a small O and he had another excuse to chide himself.

"Hi, Brian," Harper said, her tone clearly a warning. "You doing okay?"

"Yes," he answered, even though it had to be clear he wasn't. He didn't take his gaze off Emmaline. "I just want you to know I'm going back to New York on Friday."

"You're supposed to be here until the baby arrives," Harper reminded him. Emmaline still hadn't spoken.

"I'll come back. I promise." He flicked a glance at his sister-in-law. She frowned, but her gaze remained kind, like she knew how much this was killing him. Since when had he become so easy to read for people other than Brady? He didn't like it. The sense of being truly seen terrified him. "My boss needs me in the city to meet with a couple of clients."

Harper didn't look like she believed him, but Emmaline's face had gone pale. Her freckles stood out in stark relief against her skin.

"I'm sure the boys will miss you," she said after a moment.

What about you? he wanted to ask. *Will you miss me?* But he didn't say those things. Brian had made his choice after Tammy left him. He wouldn't give his heart again. Instead, he'd protect it at any cost. Emmaline needed someone different than the man he knew himself to be—she was meant for love and he was determined not to fall.

If this morning had reminded him of anything, it was that she would be fine without him. She had friends in this town, people who cared about her. She and her baby didn't need him, no matter how much he wanted them to.

"Good luck with everything," he said, as if she didn't mean the world to him. As if being apart from her wasn't shattering him.

She gave a tight nod. "You, too," she whispered.

Harper linked her arm in the crook of Emmaline's elbow. "We'll talk about this later," she told Brian with a pointed eyebrow raise.

Right. Because they were heading for Emmaline's baby shower. He could tell that his sister-in-law was growing irritated with him, and he didn't blame her. But he had to believe he was doing the right thing. He wanted what was best for Emmaline.

As much as he wanted to be that, he knew that he couldn't measure up to the kind of man she deserved to have in her life. He walked away and then deposited his muffin and the coffee cup in a nearby trash can. His stomach was tied in knots and there was no way he could eat or drink anything at the moment.

Surely the feeling would pass and he'd go back to normal.

Who was he kidding? He had no idea when or how he'd get over Emmaline, but his stomach was the least of his worries. More concerning was the fact that his heart might never recover.

Chapter Fifteen

The afternoon before he was scheduled to leave, Brian picked up Toby and Tyler from school. He'd packed snacks and driven them to the neighborhood park where they'd gone with Emmaline.

"Do you have to leave, Uncle Brian?" Tyler demanded.

Toby lined up his slingshot in front of the target, and the stone hurtled through the air and knocked over one of the aluminum cans Brian had set on a nearby fence post.

"Your aim gets better every day," he told the boy. "I'm afraid I do have to leave. By the time I come back you're going to be a regular Davy Crockett."

Toby's feathery brows drew together. "Who's Davy Cracker?"

Brian chuckled. "The original king of the wild frontier. I'll bring you a book about him when I come back," he promised.

"Will you read it to us, too?" Tyler asked him. "You do the best voices. Even better than Dad."

"We're gonna miss you," Toby added.

Brian's throat tightened at the sweetness the twins were showing him. "I'm going to miss you, too. I want to hear great reports about how you're helping your mommy while she gets ready for the baby. It's a lot of responsibility being a big brother."

Both boys went silent for several moments, which was not at all like them. Toby kicked at the ground with one sneakered foot while Tyler held so tight to the handle of the slingshot his knuckles turned white.

Brian could tell there was something they wanted to share. The question was how to get them to open up. He shook his head, wondering when he'd changed from being the uncle who fed them sugary treats for breakfast and encouraged an inordinate amount of television watching to the guy who wanted to listen and help fix their problems.

The boys shared several meaningful glances

before Toby raised his gaze to Brian's. "What if they like the new baby better?"

The words felt like an arrow straight to the heart. "Better than the two of you?" He reached out and ruffled each boy's hair. "Impossible. They will love the new baby just the right amount, but it won't affect their feelings for you at all. Your parents love you with their whole hearts."

"But we're not even their real kids," Tyler said on a rush of breath.

Where was the candy to distract everyone when Brian needed it? He knew how difficult the transition to guardian had been for Brady and the boys. It wasn't until Harper came into their lives that they'd truly become a family. Now his brother's life seemed so solid that Brian had forgotten what a new baby might represent for these boys who'd lost their mom and dad at such a young age.

He crouched down on the grass in front of the twins. "I know my brother better than almost anyone. Your mommy is probably the only person closer to him than me. We've been together since before we were even born, just like the two of you. You can believe me when I tell you that he loves you so much, and nothing is going to change that. I also have some experience with having younger siblings. They can be a pain, but they also can be lots of fun. Your new little brother or sister is going to love you and look up to you. And I promise they will be worth all the trouble in the end."

Toby nodded like what Brian was saying made perfect sense, but Tyler still frowned. "If a new baby is so great, then why aren't you staying?"

Brian wished he knew how to answer that question.

"I'll be back," he repeated. "And we're going to have a lot of fun." A familiar SUV pulled into the parking lot.

"Speaking of fun," he told the twins, "Your dad is here." Then two men got out of the vehicle. "Along with your Uncle Kane. Want me to show you how much better I am with a slingshot than either of my brothers?"

"Yes," both twins shouted at once. They ran toward Brady and Kane with renewed enthusiasm, as if their worry from a few minutes ago had never happened. Brian wished it were that easy for him to turn things on and off. Maybe then he wouldn't feel this hollow ache in his chest. It was different from the one he'd experienced when he first arrived—sharper and with jagged edges. He knew exactly where the pain came from—the hole in his heart without Emmaline in his life.

He greeted both of his brothers and immediately knew something was up. They were being far too nice to him, as if he were a fragile piece of china that might break if squeezed too hard.

He didn't like the feeling of being coddled, but at least he got the satisfaction of outperforming both of them with the slingshot. After they'd had enough of the competition, Tyler and Toby headed for the playground to get on the climbing structure and swings.

"What's going on?" Brian demanded of his brothers as soon as the twins were out of earshot.

"You belong here," Kane said without preamble.

"My life is in New York." Brian kept his tone neutral. He wasn't going to let his brothers know how hard that comment had hit him.

"Most of your family is here," Kane countered.

"All the ones that count," Brady added.

Brian shook his head. "Not going to happen, boys."

"You can't walk away from her."

Brady didn't have to name Emmaline for Brian to know who he was talking about. "I didn't walk away from her. She kicked me out."

"Because she knows you weren't in it for the long haul," Kane said.

Brady threw up his hands as he glared at Brian. "And can you blame her? She has a baby on the way. You can't mess around with a mom."

"What makes you think I was messing around?"

"We all heard you talking so proudly about your lone-wolf status."

Kane nodded in agreement. "Belle does a great impression of you howling for her."

"That was a joke." Brian looked past his brothers to where Toby and Tyler were running up the slide steps, then sliding down and jumping off only to repeat the process over and over. He wished things in his life were as simple as that. Find something that brought him joy and then just keep doing it on repeat.

Except Emmaline brought him joy. Being with her made him happy. Singing to her unborn baby gave him a sense of peace he hadn't even realized was missing in his life. Yet he was leaving.

He reminded himself that was what she wanted. He was respecting her decision by returning to his old life in New York.

"I gave her a chance to stop me." He looked back and forth between his two brothers. "I saw her in town when she and Harper were on their way to the baby shower. I told her my plan and she didn't argue. For all I know, having me out of her hair is the best idea she's heard in a long time."

"You don't believe that," Brady muttered. "Harper doesn't believe that. I don't believe that. You and Emmaline deserve each other. I've never met two more stubborn people in my life."

Brian raised a brow as Kane chuckled. "Well, I think a couple of us could give him a run for his money. But we got smart before it was too late." He pointed a finger at Brian. "Get smart."

Nerves tangled through Brian's chest. He wanted to take his brother's advice, annoying as it was. But he also didn't want to put Emmaline in a bad position. He wanted to respect her wishes, and she had clearly told him that their relationship needed to end.

"She knows I'm leaving tomorrow. Maybe she'll try to stop me."

Kane snorted. "Do you think you're going to have your Bogart-and-Bergman-in-Casablanca moment? You send her away because being a mother is greater than your feelings for her? It doesn't have to be that dramatic, Brian."

"No." Brian shook his head. "No drama and no big scenes. I'm driving back to New York, not flying, so it'd do no good for her to show up at the airport. But if she comes to the house…"

"Or you could go see her on the way out of town," Kane suggested. "Have you even told her that you love her?"

"I never said I love her." Brian ran a hand through his hair and turned away. "I've only known her for a month. People don't fall in love in such a short time."

Brady and Kane shared a look. "The smart ones do," Kane said. "When you meet the right woman, you don't worry about things like time or your pride. You take a chance."

Brady nodded. "Take a chance, Bri. You know Emmaline is worth it."

"I've got to gas up the car before I leave tomorrow and finish packing." Brian forced himself to meet his brothers' concerned gazes. "I appreciate everything you guys have said. I'm glad to see you both so happy. At this point, it isn't in the cards for me. Tell Toby and Tyler I'll see them back at the house and to prepare themselves for one more outrageous story time with Uncle Brian."

Brady's scowl softened. "Promise us that you won't be a stranger. I want all three of my kids to grow up knowing their outrageous uncle."

"Ditto," Kane said, "although Brady is way ahead of me on filling the house with kids."

Brady nodded sagely. "Let's face it. I'm an over-achiever."

Brian laughed. His twin could always make him laugh. Unfortunately, it didn't begin to soften the ache in his chest.

"But you know things haven't always been easy for me," Brady said, his tone going serious. "You might want to believe I didn't struggle, but that doesn't make it true."

Brian felt his jaw go tight. He had wanted to believe that about both of his brothers, but now he wondered if it had just been an excuse—a way to rationalize his own stupid choices in comparison.

"I was ten kinds of a mess when I became guardian of the twins."

"Understandably," Brian conceded.

"Yeah, but I almost ruined my chance with Harper because I couldn't get out of my own way."

"Same with Layla and me," Kane added. "It took a lot of effort to work it out." He held up a hand when Brian would have spoken. "It was all worth it in the end, but don't think you've got the market cornered on things not coming easy."

"Things that are worth having," Brady told him, "Often don't come easy."

Brian wondered if he'd been using easy and uncomplicated as an excuse not to put in the work. Maybe he'd done this to himself. He'd been so confident about his lone-wolf status, believing that nothing could alter his views on commitment.

Then he'd met Emmaline, and she'd changed everything. He couldn't help but secretly hope that she might stop him from leaving. Maybe he hadn't told her exactly how he felt, but he'd communicated it in other ways. At least he thought he had. All he knew was she had to be the one to reach out. His pride and fear wouldn't have it any other way.

* * *

The following morning, Emmaline climbed out of Grace's car after the other woman had parked in front of the busy barn that was hosting the estate sale. The day was slightly cloudy with the scent of rain in the air, and Emmaline was grateful for Grace's company. She might have turned off her alarm and stayed in bed all day otherwise.

"Oh, I have such a good feeling about this." Grace shielded her eyes as she studied the stream of people walking in and out of the barn with various pieces of furniture or accessories. "It feels as though we could discover something amazing. What a fun part of your job."

"It is," Emmaline said. "I used to love driving around the state with my grandfather, sourcing inventory for the shop. We'd go to estate sales and flea markets. He had a whole network of people that kept him informed about potential finds. You never knew what you were going to discover."

"So fun. I can remember walking past Rosebud Antiques as a kid and being fascinated with the window displays. Thanks for letting me tag along." Grace led the way toward the entrance. "I have a few additional pieces to get for the hotel, and I have a feeling I'll know exactly what I want when I see it."

"I'm glad for the company." Emmaline smiled, although it felt forced.

Grace immediately paused. "Brady said his brother was heading out of town this morning. You two have spent quite a bit of time together lately."

Emmaline did her best to hold her smile steady, but she knew it went wobbly. "We did. I had fun with Brian. But it was never serious." She could feel Grace studying her.

"Are you sure about that?"

Emmaline nodded. "How could it be serious when he was always planning to return to Buffalo?"

"I understand that part. When Wiley and I were first together, the plan was also for something temporary. He had his life in the big city, and I wasn't going to change him. I wasn't sure I even wanted to try."

"But something did change," Emmaline pointed out. "Wiley's here now, and the two of you are happy."

"It took both of us willing to risk having our hearts broken," Grace confirmed. "Trust me, it wasn't easy. Actually it was easy. I just didn't realize it until I decided to take the chance."

"There's a big difference then," Emmaline said. "I don't think Brian wants to risk his heart. And I've got my baby to think about. I can't allow myself to get hung up on a man who doesn't want commitment." She cradled her ever-growing belly. "I'm not really in a place to do casual long-term."

"Are you sure that's what he wants?"

"I think so." Emmaline bit down on her lower lip. In truth, she and Brian had skirted around the issue of the future so many times she couldn't say what he wanted. Yes, they'd agreed to casual and short-term but he'd treated her—and her daughter—with so much tenderness that she'd wanted to believe he'd changed.

"You don't look convinced."

Emmaline drew in a shaky breath. "I don't know. I guess I don't really know what he wants, but it's too late to find out."

"Is it?" Grace pulled her phone from the pocket of the slim cotton jacket she wore. "I have three bars of service here. You could call him."

Emmaline was tempted. Sorely tempted. What if Brian really did care about her but he thought she didn't want anything more than a temporary arrangement with him? What if she was losing her best chance at finding true love?

She gave a sharp shake of her head. She'd already told herself many times that her life could not be one of fairy tales and daydreams. She was a single mom and didn't have time for that kind of fanciful thinking. She met Grace's sympathetic gaze.

"I think if it was meant to be, I would have had a sign or something would have happened to convince both of us. Like you falling off that balcony."

Grace and Wiley had first gotten together after Grace was injured in an accident at Hotel Fortune last year. "It's great that you weren't injured, but that was a pretty big sign," Emmaline added.

Grace laughed softly. "I'm not sure I'd hold up a balcony collapse as the most romantic way to find your soul mate, but I guess it worked for me." She hugged Emmaline. "You deserve happiness, too. There is a man out there who is going to want to commit to you and your baby and give you a wonderful life filled with love."

Emmaline blinked away tears. It was still hard to imagine that life with anyone but Brian.

"I hope you're right," she said, then glanced over as a woman carried out a gilded mirror that would have been perfect for one of her clients. "Right now, let's get into the sale before we miss this opportunity as well."

They wandered into the barn, which had been transformed into rows of tables holding household goods, with pieces of furniture lining the perimeter.

"This is amazing," Grace murmured.

"Yeah." Emmaline reached for the feeling of anticipation and excitement these kinds of events normally brought her, but it was hard to feel anything past missing Brian. Had he left yet? Was he speeding away from town and her even as she thought about him? How would he respond if she reached out to him now?

She put those thoughts aside as she and Grace perused the aisles. Grace stopped to talk to one of the estate sale managers while Emmaline continued toward the back of the barn.

There were tables and chairs pushed against the wall and a row of built-in shelves that held various pieces of china, lamps and accessories.

On the top of one high shelf, she noticed a corner of what looked like another mirror with a tarnished gold frame. Maybe she hadn't missed her chance at getting the perfect piece for her client after all.

She looked for one of the young men who was helping customers move items, but there was no one nearby. It felt as though the people in the barn around her were on some sort of buying frenzy. Everywhere she looked, other customers were hauling items to the cash register area. Emmaline was afraid to walk away from the shelf on the off chance that someone would grab the mirror before she could get back.

After another thorough look for a worker she could flag down, she turned back to the shelf. There was a sturdy table just to the side of it, and she figured she could at least check out the piece to see if it was really as perfect as that corner led her to believe. She placed her purse on a nearby chair and hefted herself up on the table.

She made sure to be careful and go slow because her belly was starting to throw off her balance a bit. But she could still manage it and counseled herself that it was smart to push herself. There was going to be nobody to help her on a regular basis, so she had to keep doing things for herself.

She reached for the mirror but noticed it had a crack running from one corner to the other. The frame was gorgeous but not worth the trouble if the mirror wasn't also in good shape. She took a step back but her heel caught on the corner of the table. She'd shifted farther to the right than she'd realized and quickly pinwheeled her arms to try to gain her balance.

She heard Grace call out her name and instinctively turned, but that only pitched her even more off balance. A scream split the dusty air of the barn, and she realized it had come from her. There was the feeling of weightlessness, like she was floating on a cloud, and then a split second of understanding that she wasn't floating. She was falling.

Then she hit the ground and everything went black.

Chapter Sixteen

Brian flipped the radio on and off as he drove through the open plains of East Texas. The silence was no good because it left him with only his thoughts, which were a montage of moments he'd spent with Emmaline and how much he was going to miss her. The radio did no good because every song seemed to remind him of her or their trip to Austin together, which left him fidgety and frustrated.

He'd gotten on the road an hour after he'd planned that morning because he'd dillydallied, secretly hoping she might show up at Brady's house and stop him. That would prove she was really choosing him. It would prove he was worth the effort of something more than casual.

He wasn't surprised she hadn't shown up.

He adjusted the vent on the dash. He couldn't seem to make the temperature in his vehicle comfortable either. Cold sweat dribbled between his shoulder blades.

His phone rang, and he startled. He'd had patchy service for the past hour and frowned as he picked up the phone and saw Brady's number as well as four missed calls that had come in.

"What's going on?" he asked as he hit the accept button.

"Where are you?" Brady asked. His voice filled the quiet interior of the car, thanks to Bluetooth.

"In the middle of nowhere, from the looks of it. What's wrong? Is it Harper? Do you need—"

"It's Emmaline."

Brian immediately swerved off the two-lane highway, sending up a cloud of dust and gravel. "What about Emmaline?"

"How fast can you get back here?"

Brian let out a string of curses that would have had his mother threatening to wash his mouth out with soap. "Tell me what's happening. Is it the baby? Is she okay?"

There was a beat of silence. Brian picked up his

phone, cursing again when he noticed he'd gone down to just a single bar of service.

"I don't know," Brady said after a moment. "I got a call from Grace that Emmaline had been injured in a fall."

"What kind of fall? At the hotel? Is she okay, Brady?"

"I don't know the answer to anything you're asking. Harper said she was going to the hospital with Emmaline, but she hasn't called again. I think I would have heard if something bad happened. Maybe I shouldn't have called you. This isn't your problem anymore. I know that. I'll let you know when I hear more."

"I'm turning around." Brian yanked the steering wheel and skidded onto the highway back toward Rambling Rose with another spray of gravel. "Call me if you hear anything or have updates. Can you try to get her mom's number? Emmaline would want her to know if she doesn't already."

"Are you sure about this?" Brady asked, his tone still tense but somewhat quieter. "Calling you was my gut instinct, but now I wonder—"

"You were right to call." Brian squeezed shut his eyes for just a moment and gripped the steering wheel more tightly. He shouldn't have walked away and would never forgive himself if Emmaline lost—

No. He couldn't even go there. His brother had reached out for a reason, and Brian wasn't going to be fool enough not to try for another chance. "You were right about everything, and don't ask me to repeat myself because it kills me to say it once. I'll get there as soon as I can." He drew in a shaky breath. "She has to be okay, Brady."

"I know," his brother agreed. "I know."

Brian made it to the community hospital in Rambling Rose in record time. He didn't even want to think what might have happened if he'd been pulled over for speeding. But a ticket was nothing compared to his worry over Emmaline.

Brady had texted him with Krista's number, but she hadn't picked up when he called. He'd also called the reception desk at the hospital, but they hadn't been willing to give him any information. Brady hadn't heard from Harper, so Brian was going in blind.

All he had was his love for Emmaline and the faith that he could get her through anything. He would be the man she deserved if he had to spend the rest of his life working to get there.

All of the doubts and questions that had plagued him over the past month seemed stupid and silly in hindsight.

She was his person. His home. It didn't matter

if they were here or in New York or Timbuktu. He'd been stupid enough to turn his back on the woman of his dreams because he was afraid of getting hurt.

But that pain was nothing in comparison to the razor-sharp ache of not being with her when she needed him.

Or maybe she didn't need him. Despite her soft-spoken demeanor and some of her insecurities, Emmaline was the most staunchly independent and self-sufficient person he'd ever met.

It terrified him but, at the same time, was one of the characteristics he loved best about her.

He headed straight for the information desk and asked about her. The older woman sitting behind the large computer monitor gave him a wary stare. He could imagine how frenzied he looked, at least based on how frenzied he felt.

"Brian."

He turned to see Emmaline's mom approaching from the hallway that led to the cafeteria, a tray of food in her hands.

"How is she? Can I see her?" He ran a hand through his hair and tried to manage his rising panic. "Please."

Krista stared at him for several seconds, her mouth a thin, disapproving line.

"I love her," he blurted. "I'm sorry I didn't tell

her sooner. I'm sorry I let her believe I wanted things to be casual. Casual is the last thing I want from your daughter, Ms. Lewis. I know I've messed up, but I'm going to make it up to her. I promise. If only she'll give me a chance. And you'll give me a chance. Please tell me she's okay."

Krista's eyes bore into his for what seemed an eternity, then finally she spoke. "Come with me," she said, her tone giving away nothing.

He wanted to know what he was walking into. To ask questions and get a sense of Emmaline's condition and what they were up against. Then he realized it didn't matter. Whatever Emmaline was facing or however serious the fall had been, Brian wanted to be a part of her life. He wanted to help her cope with whatever came their way.

He still wished her mother would say something, but they walked down the hall in silence. She eventually stopped in front of a room with the door shut and turned to him. "My daughter is special," she said.

He nodded in agreement. "She's the best person I know."

"Emmaline has a big heart. She always has. Her grandfather absolutely adored her. I'm grateful for it because I didn't do the best job of bringing men into her life who deserved to be there."

"I'm sure you did your best," Brian said. "I know Emmaline thinks the world of you."

Krista inclined her head. "As I said, my daughter has a big heart. She hides it sometimes or pretends to not need anyone, but I don't want her to have to do that. I want her to be with somebody who appreciates who she is and doesn't try to turn her into somebody else or make her feel small."

"I don't want to make her feel small," Brian said quietly. "I understand my recent actions might not lead you to believe that, but I have so much respect for Emmaline. For the choices she's made and her big heart and her place in this community. If she lets me back into her life, I promise I'll show you both how much I care about her."

He wasn't sure if anything he was saying made sense, but her mother nodded. Then she handed him the tray of food and opened the door to the hospital room so that he could enter. Emmaline was in the bed, propped up by pillows with her eyes closed. There was a faint bruise on her temple and she was hooked up to some sort of monitor. She looked so peaceful that he couldn't believe something was really wrong. Or maybe he just didn't want to believe it.

As the door shut behind him, he glanced over his shoulder and noticed that her mother hadn't followed him in. When he turned back, Emmaline was staring at him. Was it just his imagination or did she look slightly paler than she had seconds earlier?

"I thought you'd be at least to the Oklahoma border by now," she said.

"Brady called me. He said you'd been in an accident. I came back."

"And you brought Jell-O." One corner of her mouth lifted, although her eyes still looked sad. "I'm sorry your trip was impacted by me."

"Emmaline, are you, okay?" He placed the tray on the table next to her bed. He wanted to reach for her but was too afraid of how she might react. "Is the baby…?"

She placed both hands on her belly, then gestured to the monitor quietly beeping next to her. "Her heartbeat is steady."

"Your arm…" he murmured, noticing that her left arm was enveloped in a sling and tucked close to her body.

She looked down at her arm as well. "It's just a wrist sprain. I was reaching for something on a high shelf at the estate sale Grace and I went to this morning. It was stupid of me, but I'm fine. We're fine. The doctor wants to monitor the baby for a while longer and then we'll go home."

Brian lowered himself onto the chair next to the bed because it felt like his knees might give out. He was so relieved she and the baby were fine. Also, his knees might be weak, thanks to nerves, as he thought about what he wanted to say to her now. And what her reaction might be.

Emmaline picked up the bowl of Jell-O and reached for a spoon, but her injured arm bumped it and knocked it to the floor.

"I'll get you another one." Brian immediately stood. "What else do you need? I'll get anything you need."

He didn't care if it was a spoon or a trip to the moon, Brian would do whatever it took to prove to her that he deserved another chance. It meant risking his heart, but Emmaline was worth it. She was worth everything he had to give.

Emmaline wasn't sure what it meant that Brian had returned. Were they friends still? Did he have some misplaced sense of guilt or chivalry when it came to her? Emotions stampeded across her heart, hope and fear warring for dominance. It was easier to deal with the mundane details than try to unwind the tangle of unspoken questions between them.

"There are extras in the nightstand." She smiled as he handed her another spoon. Her stomach was way too shaky to even think of taking a bite. "It was nice of you to come back," she told him even though nice was a wholly inappropriate word for the emotions cascading through her. In the moment after her fall, when she was being raced to the hospital in an ambulance due to her pregnancy, all Emmaline could think of was that she wanted Brian with her.

She wanted him with her for the hard times and the happy moments. She'd been so busy protecting her heart from being hurt that she hadn't given their relationship a real chance. She wanted another chance. She wanted to believe he'd turned around not because of some chivalrous sense of duty or because his brother had pressured him into it. Was it possible that he'd realized the same thing as her?

"I'm sorry if I put you behind schedule to get back to New York."

"Don't apologize. This is where I want to be. It's where I should have been this whole time."

Emmaline drew in a breath as hope spiraled through her.

"I need to tell you something," they said at the exact same time.

Emmaline smiled and did her best not to squeeze the Jell-O cup so tightly that it exploded all over the place. Her nerves were running on overdrive at the moment.

"You first," Brian said, then shook his head and

got up, pacing from one end of the room to the other. "Can I go first? Because I'm afraid I won't have the guts to tell you what I want to say if you try to send me away."

The last thing Emmaline wanted at this point was to send Brian away, but she couldn't seem to form the words to tell him that. So she nodded, then mumbled, "You first."

He stared at her for a long moment, and she got the impression that he was trying to memorize her face. She hoped that didn't mean he was leaving again. She hoped that if this was another goodbye she had the strength to make it through.

"I love you, Emmaline." His voice was thick with emotion. "I can't explain it and I don't even want to try. From the moment I saw you on New Year's Eve, I felt a connection different from anything I've ever experienced. You are smart and beautiful and you care about the people around you so deeply. More than anything, I want to be one of those people."

"What happened to casual?" she asked, her voice hoarse.

"That was an excuse. A stupid, cowardly excuse because I'm afraid of the power you have over me."

She laughed at that. "I doubt I have much power over you."

He came to the side of the bed and sat next

to her. "I'm yours," he told her. The intensity in his gaze made her breath catch. "I think I was yours from the first time we met. You are my person. I understand if you don't want to give me another chance. I know I've made a complete mess of things. But if you do, I promise I'll do better. I promise I'll spend the rest of our lives proving that I deserve you."

He ran a hand through his hair. "Scratch that last part. I'll probably never deserve someone as amazing as you, Emmaline. But I'll never stop trying. I want to make you happy. I want to be with you."

Tears clogged her throat. She needed to hear those words from him, and she wanted to believe it. She wanted to trust him. But she wasn't the only person involved right now.

"It's not just me, Brian." She touched a hand to her belly once again. "I'm a package deal. I know that's a lot. I don't expect you to—"

"I want to." He covered her hand with his. "I want to take care of your baby. I want to be a father. The whole bit. I want to change diapers and sing lullabies in the middle of the night when she can't sleep. I want to go to every elementary school concert she has and coach soccer or swimming or whatever she wants to do. I want to stand at the front door when her first boyfriend picks her up, and I want to scare the hell out of him because she's my daughter, and I love her. I love her already, Em. Just like I love you. Oh, God, you're crying. Why are you crying?" He started to pull his hand away, but she held tight.

"They're happy tears," she said. "Because I love you, too, Brian."

The baby kicked as she said the words. "I'm pretty sure she loves you, too. All I could think of today was that I wanted you with me. For all of it. It's hard for me to let people in. But somehow you snuck around every defensive wall I had."

"I've always been the sneaky twin," he said with a shaky laugh.

"You're mine," she told him. She sat up straighter and cupped his cheek with her free hand. "I love you, Brian Fortune. I want to let you in. Heck, you're already in. Are we really going to do this? Are you sure?"

He gave her a solemn nod and then dropped to one knee at the side of the bed.

"What are you doing?" Emmaline felt her eyes grow wide and dashed a hand over her cheeks.

"Emmaline Lewis"—he glanced at her belly—"and sweet baby girl, would you do me the honor of becoming my family? Will you marry me, Em?"

"Yes," Emmaline whispered.

He kissed her, and it felt like coming home.

Brian was her home. He was everything she wanted and she knew they would be happy together for the rest of their lives. No matter what happened. No matter what they faced, they would do it together.

A knock sounded at the door and they both glanced up to see Harper peeking in. Her eyes widened at the sight of Emmaline's tear-stained face. "Is everything okay?"

"Better than." Brian grinned ear to ear. "Emmaline said yes."

Brady appeared at the doorway next to his wife. "You should have listened to me sooner, bro. I'm always right."

Emmaline laughed as Brian offered his brother a jovial one-finger salute. Then Harper and Brady entered the room followed by Emmaline's mother, who gave her a tight hug.

"I'm so happy for you," she said into Emmaline's ear.

Emmaline was so happy. And she knew somehow that her grandfather was happy for her as well. She had the sense that he was watching over her and her baby and now Brian. Looking out for her family and her heart.

Epilogue

Emmaline smiled when Brian took her hand as he turned onto the road that led toward town. She was smiling a lot lately. The past week had been the best she could remember and she had a feeling things would just keep getting better.

"I think I should trade in this car for a minivan," he said, giving her fingers a squeeze.

She snorted out a soft laugh, then realized he was serious. "You're going to go from driving a BMW to a minivan?"

"Have you seen those things lately? I was doing some research online. They have so many bells and whistles, and the safety ratings are amazing."

"Safety ratings," she repeated. "This sedan is plenty safe, Brian. Plus, I think a car seat will fit fine in here. I know babies cause a mess and you probably just got your car clean after the twins—"

"Em, I don't care about the mess. I welcome the mess. The messier the better. I'm in it for everything."

She nodded. "I know. And I appreciate that. I love you, Brian."

"I love you, too, and I love our baby." He flashed a sheepish grin. "I love the little brothers and sisters that I want her to have someday. I'm in for all of it."

Emmaline's heart seemed to glow so bright she felt like she could see the light from it coming out of her chest. It had taken her a bit to trust that Brian was as dedicated as he claimed. But she knew without a doubt that he meant every word he said.

He pulled to a stop at a red light and turned to her. "Show me the picture again."

She held up the piece of photo paper with the image from the ultrasound she'd just had. Their baby was healthy and growing and it was everything Emmaline wanted for her future.

"She is gorgeous," Brian murmured. "We haven't talked about names. Do you have something in mind?"

"Allie," Emmaline whispered. "I was thinking of calling her Allie after my grandfather."

"Allie for her great-grandpa Albert." Brian nodded. "It's perfect."

"It was Harper and Brady who gave me the idea." Harper had given birth to a perfect baby girl a few days earlier and they'd named her Brenda after her maternal grandmother. Emmaline grinned. "I just know our girls are going to be best friends."

"Of course they are. The twins are almost as excited to meet their new cousin as they were to meet their baby sister."

"You helped them a lot with that. You're a great uncle, and I know you're going be a wonderful father."

"Especially tooling around town in my minivan," he said and she laughed.

"Whatever makes you happy."

"You make me happy. Happier than I feel like I have a right to be." He pulled into an empty space in front of the antique shop.

"We both got the exact right amount of happiness," she assured him. "I don't take that for granted."

"Me neither." He hopped out of the car and quickly went to her side to open the door. She appreciated the way he took care of her and also that he supported her independence and her dedication to the shop.

Brian had moved into the apartment with her after returning, and they were currently shopping for a house. Neither one of them was in any hurry to leave behind their cozy apartment. Emmaline knew without a doubt that no matter where they lived it would be home because they would be together.

They walked into the shop, and she flipped the open sign while Brian gathered the mail that had been delivered through the slot next to the front door.

"There's something addressed to me." He frowned. "I must be official if I'm getting mail at the store."

"Officially the best thing that's ever happened to me. Who's it from?"

He broke the seal on the manila envelope. "There's no return address." His eyes widened as he pulled out a slip of paper and scanned it. "It's a letter giving me official access to the safe deposit box in Austin."

"The key from the horse sculpture?" Emmaline turned to where the piece of art sat on a shelf behind the cash register. They'd never solved the mystery of it, and she'd continued to wonder about the sculpture's origins, the cryptic message on the plaque at the base and what it all meant.

"There's another slip of paper in here." He reached a hand into the envelope once more, his brows furrowing as he read the message. "What do you make of this?" He handed the note to Emmaline.

"'The Key to the Future,'" she read aloud. "It has to be referring to the safe deposit box but there's no note. Maybe there's something inside it that will tell us more."

Brian nodded, an excited gleam in his gaze as it held hers. "Are you up for another visit to Austin?"

Emmaline pressed a hand to her belly as Allie kicked inside her. "I think we both are." She took a step closer to Brian and wound her arms around his neck. "You know how you've wanted to get married right away?"

"Today," he answered without hesitation. "We can go to the courthouse today. Tomorrow. Whenever you'll make an honest man of me, Em. I want to be your husband."

She stood on her tiptoes and brushed a kiss over his mouth. "I think Austin would be a wonderful location for a wedding." She deepened the kiss. "And a mini-honeymoon," she said after a moment.

He gave a loud whoop of delight and spun her in a circle. "Looks like I owe Alonzo Flynn's sculpture a huge debt of gratitude. That horse changed everything for me." He lowered her to her feet and nuzzled her neck. "You changed everything, Em. I love you, and tomorrow, I'm going to promise to love and honor you for the rest of my life."

Emmaline sighed and leaned into his embrace, her heart full and at peace. She'd found her person in Brian and knew they would build a life to remember together in Rambling Rose.

* * * * *

Look for the next book in the new
Harlequin Special Edition continuity
The Fortunes of Texas: The Wedding Gift

A Soldier's Dare
by Jo McNally

On sale February 2022 wherever
Harlequin books and ebooks are sold.

**WE HOPE YOU ENJOYED
THIS BOOK FROM**

**H HARLEQUIN
SPECIAL
EDITION**

Believe in love. Overcome obstacles. Find happiness.

Relate to finding comfort and strength in the
support of loved ones and enjoy the journey
no matter what life throws your way.

6 NEW BOOKS AVAILABLE EVERY MONTH!

COMING NEXT MONTH FROM

◆ HARLEQUIN
SPECIAL EDITION

#2887 A SOLDIER'S DARE
The Fortunes of Texas: The Wedding Gift • by Jo McNally
When Jack Radcliffe dares Belle Fortune to kiss him at the Hotel Fortune's
Valentine's Ball, he thinks he's just having fun. She's interested in someone else.
But from the moment their lips touch, the ex-military man is in trouble. The woman
he shouldn't want challenges him to confront his painful past—and face his future
head-on...

#2888 HER WYOMING VALENTINE WISH
Return to the Double C • by Allison Leigh
When Delia Templeton is tapped to run her wealthy grandmother's new charitable
foundation, she finds herself dealing with Mac Jeffries, the stranger who gave her a
bracing New Year's kiss. Working together gives Delia and Mac ample opportunity
to butt heads...and revisit that first kiss as Valentine's Day fast approaches...

#2889 STARLIGHT AND THE SINGLE DAD
Welcome to Starlight • by Michelle Major
Relocating to the Cascade Mountains is the first step in Tessa Reynolds's plan to
reinvent herself. Former military pilot Carson Campbell sees the bold and beautiful
redhead only wreaking havoc with his own plan to be the father his young daughter
needs. As her feelings for Carson deepen, Tessa finally knows who she wants to
be—the woman who walks off with Carson's heart...

#2890 THE SHOE DIARIES
The Friendship Chronicles • by Darby Baham
From the outside, Reagan "Rae" Doucet has it all: a coveted career in
Washington, DC, a tight circle of friends and a shoe closet to die for. When one of
her crew falls ill, however, Rae is done playing it safe. The talented but unfulfilled
writer makes a "risk list" to revamp her life. But forgiving her ex, Jake Saunders,
might be one risk too many...

#2891 THE FIVE-DAY REUNION
Once Upon a Wedding • by Mona Shroff
Law student Anita Virani hasn't seen her ex-husband since the divorce. Now she's
agreed to pretend she's still married to Nikhil until his sister's wedding celebrations
are over—because her former mother-in-law neglected to tell her family of their split!

#2892 THE MARINE'S RELUCTANT RETURN
The Stirling Ranch • by Sabrina York
She'd been the girl he'd always loved—until she married his best friend. Now
Crystal Stoker was a widowed single mom and Luke Stirling was trying his best
to avoid her. That was proving impossible in their small town. The injured marine
was just looking for a little peace and quiet, not expecting any second chances,
especially ones he didn't dare accept.

**YOU CAN FIND MORE INFORMATION ON UPCOMING HARLEQUIN TITLES,
FREE EXCERPTS AND MORE AT HARLEQUIN.COM.**

HSECNM0122A

"I won! I won!"

"That you did," he said, laughing and trying to climb
out of his own tube. With his long legs, he was having
a hard time getting out on his own, so I reached out my
hand to help him up. As soon as he grabbed me, we both
went soaring, feet away from the slides. I was amazed
neither of us fell onto the ground, but I think just when
we were about to, he caught me midair and steadied us.

"Okay, so a deal is a deal. Truth. Do you like me?"

"I can't believe you wasted your truth on something
you already know."

"Maybe a girl needs to hear it sometimes."

"Reagan Doucet, I will tell you all day long how much
I like you," he said, bending down again so he could

stare directly into my eyes. "But you have to believe me when I do. No more of that 'c'mon, Jake' stuff. You either believe me or you don't."

"Deal," I said, grabbing hold of the loops on the waist of his pants to bring him even closer to me. "You got it."

"Mmm, no. I've got you," he whispered, bringing his lips centimeters away from mine but refusing to kiss me. Instead, he stood there, making me wait, and then flicked out his tongue with a grin, barely scraping the skin on my lips. It was clear Jake wanted me to want him. Better yet, crave him. And while I could also tell this was him putting on his charm armor again, I didn't care. I was in shoe, Christmas lights and sexy guy heaven, and for once I was determined to enjoy it. Not much could top that.

"Now, let's go find these pandas."

I reached out my hand, and he took it as we went skipping to the next exhibit.

Don't miss The Shoe Diaries *by Darby Baham,*
available February 2022 wherever
Harlequin Special Edition books and ebooks are sold.

Harlequin.com